"I'LI

Tracy

He almost let her go. Almost decided to leave things the way they were, but she turned, the moonlight slid across her face and he saw the bleak emotion in her eyes. "Ah, Tracy," he whispered, then fit his hand around her nape under her thick braid and drew her toward him, running his thumb over the silken curve of her cheek. "Not like that," he murmured, "I can't leave you looking like that."

She tried to smile, but his tenderness shattered her, made her tremble, brought an uncontrollable sob from her chest.

"Let me help, Tracy," Don said softly.

To her dismay, tears spurted out, and she squeezed her eyes shut to block others, but they broke free and splashed down her cheek. She hadn't let herself cry in years, not even when her mother had died. "Why did you have to come back?"

He smiled as he wiped the tears from her face. "I came back for you, Tracy. I mean to have you. In every way there is. And you know it's going to happen. . . ."

WHAT ARE *LOVESWEPT* ROMANCES?

They are stories of true romance and touching emotion. We believe those two very important ingredients are constants in our highly sensual and very believable stories in the LOVESWEPT *line. Our goal is to give you, the reader, stories of consistently high quality that may sometimes make you laugh, sometimes make you cry, but are always fresh and creative and contain many delightful surprises within their pages.*

Most romance fans read an enormous number of books. Those they truly love, they keep. Others may be traded with friends and soon forgotten. We hope that each LOVESWEPT *romance will be a treasure—a "keeper." We will always try to publish*

LOVE STORIES YOU'LL NEVER FORGET
BY AUTHORS YOU'LL ALWAYS REMEMBER

The Editors

Loveswept® 733

SIREN SONG

JUDY GILL

BANTAM BOOKS
NEW YORK · TORONTO · LONDON · SYDNEY · AUCKLAND

SIREN SONG
A Bantam Book / March 1995

ISBN 0-553-44456-5

Published simultaneously in the United States and Canada

Bantam Books are published by Bantam Books, a division of Bantam Doubleday Dell Publishing Group, Inc. Its trademark, consisting of the words "Bantam Books" and the portrayal of a rooster, is Registered in U.S. Patent and Trademark Office and in other countries. Marca Registrada. Bantam Books, 1540 Broadway, New York, New York 10036.

PRINTED IN THE UNITED STATES OF AMERICA

OPM 0 9 8 7 6 5 4 3 2 1

ONE

It was a form of insanity, Don figured, the leading edge of his midlife crisis. From the moment he'd seen Professor Maxwell's grant application, he'd been able to think of nothing but returning to Blackfish Island in Johnstone Strait—and to the scene of an event that for years he had managed to keep out of his conscious mind.

He wondered if he would have come back even if the board hadn't approved Professor Maxwell's grant. As a member of that board, he'd abstained from the vote, claiming a conflict of interest because he'd once worked under the professor. That was the proper procedure, tradition. It was also tradition that each applicant who won a grant receive the news directly from a member of the five-person board. Those visits were always made in strict rotation.

He knew the traditions and procedures as well as anyone; he'd worked for the foundation for nearly five years. Yet, once the vote was in, he'd shamelessly finagled his way out of the set order and begged from the director the privilege of conveying the good news to Blackfish Island Orca Research Station himself. He still wondered how much of that decision had come from his desire to revisit BIO Research and his old professor, and how much from his steadily growing itch to renew the acquaintance of the professor's daughter.

One brief meeting six years earlier had brought back memories now fifteen years old. The professor's grant application had simply intensified them.

He sighed. Did all men his age find themselves harking back to the follies of their youth? It was some kind of masochism, he suspected, the way he let her image continue to haunt him.

Tall and wand-slim she'd been, a girl too young for him to touch. Sleek and firm and strong, with eyes that could be fiery one second and darkly moody the next, and a red, pouting mouth that begged to be kissed, molded, taught. She'd come to him with a body ripe with hot young hormones aching to be channeled, and the kind of determination that just wouldn't take no for an answer, regardless of how tactful he'd tried to be. Finally, he'd decided that what tact had failed to accomplish, a good scare might. His actions had backfired on him so badly, he'd thought he'd never recover from the need that one kiss had loosed within him.

For years he'd tucked the memories, along with the shame, deep into a corner of his mind, as he'd tucked one small photograph deep into the recesses of a book he never read.

Until he'd seen her six years before. Then he'd opened the book unerringly at the right page to find her picture.

He gripped the hard plastic of the steering wheel as he directed the boat across the choppy water, steering around Griffith Point, which jutted in a southeasterly direction like a thumb stretched away from the half-closed fist that was Blackfish Island. In the lee of the point, the water was calm, mirroring the golden, mossy bluffs of the shore. Tall cedars surmounted the island, a backdrop for the low, sprawling house set above the shore halfway between the base of the "thumb" and Lyon Head, which formed the bent knuckle of the "index finger." Even after a fifteen-year absence, he felt a sweeping sense of familiarity and automatically veered wide to avoid the kelp bed marking a reef he'd once piled a boat onto.

He slowed as he approached the wharf and scowled. The entire place looked deserted; no boats tied up or anchored out in the bay, no activity onshore, no groups of students willingly attending to chores in exchange for the privilege of living with orcas in the wild. This time of year, the place should have been swarming in anticipation of the whales arriving, if they hadn't already done so. Where was everyone?

He scanned the windows of the house, seeing only silver-blue glints of reflected ocean, no curious faces, no hand lifted in greeting. No big golden retriever came lolloping across the sloping grounds, tail wagging as it ran. Of course not. Fifteen years had passed. The dog was long gone. Yet the passage of time couldn't account for the doors that stood closed on sheds and workshops, and on the boathouse at the head of the bay.

Tracy heard the approaching outboard and felt a chill prickle her arms despite the warm mid-June afternoon. A glance out the window showed a rental boat with the markings of a Malcolm Island fishing charter company heading her way. Her heart stopped for a second, and her knees went momentarily weak. She'd tried to hope it was all a mistake, but it was true. Don Jacobs really was coming. In fact, he was nearly there. Not for a second did she entertain a hope that boat carried anyone else, like a lost fisherman or a curious tourist. The Fuller Brush man.

Her luck hadn't been that good in recent years.

She had no idea why he was coming to BIO Research Station. His secretary, when she'd called that morning, had said only that he was "expected" at their station sometime that day, which Tracy knew to be patently untrue. No one was expected there. She took great care to keep unexpected visitors from turning up.

She had been too stunned to ask for details and was only grateful that the woman *had* called, that she'd had those few hours' warning.

It had been long enough to get her sister, Edie, and her father safely away.

Siren Song

5

The tone of the outboard changed from high-pitched whine to low rumble, and she ran to the corner windows for a better view inside the bay. The boat's bow had dropped, its rooster tail died down. She pulled in a long, unsteady breath as she saw sunlight glint on blond hair highlighted against blue water.

Oh, yes. There was no doubt about it. That was definitely Don Jacobs standing behind the wheel, head and shoulders over the windshield, face turned shoreward as if he were scanning for a sign of human habitation. If he found none, wouldn't he simply leave?

Now, there was a thought. She and Con could hide, pretend there was no one home.

The idea made her smile. Hide Con? Fat chance of that. First, it would take a large dose of anesthetic administered with a dart gun from a long range. Con was not the kind of woman who'd ever consider hiding an option. If it had been up to her, Edie and the professor would still be there, and the three of them would be taking on Don Jacobs as a united front. Con would have no part of hiding, no part of pretending, but since Tracy was calling the shots . . .

She stepped outside. For a moment her mouth went dry, but she squared her shoulders and told herself she was more than ready to see him.

Tracy Maxwell would not be daunted by a man or by a memory. *She* daunted *men.* Six years earlier, she'd seen Don Jacobs react to her the way most men did. Their reunion had been brief and casual, as well as overseen by her father, but she had known. She'd seen it in his eyes—regret for what he had passed up, a surge of renewed interest, and a brief, swiftly hidden wish to do it all over again differently. Which, of course, his strong sense of morality wouldn't permit.

All she needed to do was remember that, keep it firmly in the front of her mind. Besides, Donald Jacobs would not be staying long. She'd promised her sister, and she always kept her promises.

Tilting her chin, she sauntered along the path toward the ramp leading to the wharf. She grinned. "Look out, Jacobs, here I come," she said softly as the boat sidled up to the float. "Here I come, and away you go."

If he didn't bow out on his own bat the moment she said that her father wasn't available, then she had a surefire plan to get rid of him. All she needed to do was keep her wits about her and she'd win this round.

She wiped damp palms over the wisps of hair escaping her braid, and stuffed suddenly trembly fingers into the front pockets of her black jeans. Don stepped out of the boat, looked up at her as she descended the ramp, then simply stood there and stared.

"Maxwell one, Jacobs zip," Tracy murmured, and strode along the dock to greet him.

As he stepped onto the dock Don saw her swinging toward him, the bright sun pouring down on the richness of her dark brown hair, turning her skin to golden cream. *Tracy!* Everything within him came to a sudden halt, waiting for the world to catch up.

She moved with loose-limbed confidence, her legs

swinging gracefully, her arms bent at the elbows, fingers tucked into the front pockets of her jeans, throwing her breasts into relief within a red T-shirt emblazoned with leaping orcas and the station logo. He stood watching her, the rope loose and unforgotten in his hand, and didn't move.

He couldn't move.

At sixteen she'd been pretty, disturbingly so. At twenty-five she'd been stunning, not classically beautiful, but immensely attractive and appealing. And now, as she approached thirty-one . . . Words failed him.

Then she was before him, a smile on her lips, her hand extended. He thought he detected a whiff of her scent.

He took her hand, finding it strong and cool within his clasp. He forced himself to do nothing more than grip it with gentle firmness as he fought down the urge to pull it up to his face, place his mouth in the center of her palm, and—

"Tracy . . ." he said, trying not to reveal how bowled over he felt. His reaction to her filled his throat with a thickness that precluded more than the uttering of her name.

As if totally unaware of his emotional disarray, she continued to smile at him, her chocolate-colored eyes bright and welcoming, and her lips, still plump, still red, still as tempting as sin, half-parted. Her heavy dark bangs fell in a deep wave over her broad forehead, half obscuring one eye until she tossed them impatiently aside, a mannerism that was pure Tracy. It made him break into a smile that felt big and loose and inane on his face.

"Hello, Don," she said, and her warm, husky voice filled him.

"Tracy," he said again.

"Welcome back to BIO Research."

For a moment Tracy could say nothing more than that; she could only stare into his eyes, caught by the novelty of looking *up* at a man, and feel the hard warmth of his hand wrapped around hers until she remembered to pull it free. The sun gleamed in the burnished gold of his hair, imparting a dozen different shades to the full, thick strands, not one of which was gray.

The man is over forty, she'd blithely told her sister that morning. *He'll be bald, paunchy, and wearing thick glasses.*

Wrong-o, Trace! No balding, no paunch. No thick glasses.

Why had she expected it? Six years before he'd been much the same as he was now. The only hint that time had passed was the deepened laugh lines around his mouth and eyes. She reminded herself that fair-haired men seldom showed their age. She shouldn't have forgotten that. She shouldn't have tried to forget, not for a minute, the impact he could have on her.

His eyes, chips of bright blue, squinted against the sun dazzle off the water, traveled over her with slow, deliberate intent as if he were searching for changes, differences—improvements? Suddenly, for one bad moment, his scrutiny left her feeling gawky, ugly, rangy, and much too tall. In that instant years of ego-enhancing masculine appreciation were whipped away, leaving only bitter memories of rejection. It made breathing difficult. She dropped her gaze.

"It's good to see you, Tracy," he said.

As swiftly as it had come over her, her awkwardness was gone and she was once more in control of herself. "Thanks. It's good to see you too," she said, continuing to meet his gaze until she felt giddy. Swiftly, she dropped her lashes and crouched to tie the bow line.

Taking her cue, Don finally remembered the rope he still held in one hand and tied it to a ring on the edge of the float. "I . . . didn't really expect you to be here," he said, standing erect. He wished his voice had come out stronger, not so close to a raspy whisper, but it was all he could achieve at the moment. Why, when he remembered everything else about her, had he forgotten the things she could do with those lashes of hers?

"I'm so sorry," she said, rising and brushing off her hands. "I know you expected to see my father."

He drew a blank for a moment, feeling unexpectedly gauche and ill at ease. Her father? Oh! Of course. He'd come to see the professor. He frowned. That was something to remember. He had, in his official capacity, come to see Professor Maxwell. Focusing on that might help nullify Tracy Maxwell's devastating effect on his equilibrium. Sex appeal. That was it. She had incredible sex appeal.

Fifteen years earlier, he'd reacted the same way at

his first meeting with her, hadn't he? And again six years later. Why had he hoped, even faintly, that it would be different this time? And he'd been wrong: If hope equaled expectation, then he'd expected her to be there.

"It's a pity you came all this way, only to be disappointed," she said. She looked so earnest, he had to smile again, and then he gave in to temptation.

He touched her—a knuckle bent to follow the delicate line of her jaw. "Did I say I was disappointed?"

She looked down, then back up quickly, a soft smile on her lips, an oddly—and charmingly—shy light in her eyes, and a pair of pink patches on her cheeks. For an instant she looked so much like the girl he remembered, he felt guilty for touching her.

"No, of course not," she said. "I'm sure you're too tactful for that. But what I'm trying to say is that it's too bad you didn't let Dad know you were coming. I know he'd have loved to see you."

Don frowned again. "I did let him know I was coming. We spoke on the phone in early February and chose this as a time when both my schedule and his would be clear—and there'd likely be whales congregating in the strait."

Tracy could scarcely believe him—except there was no reason not to believe him. Why would he lie about it? And Dad might have called Don, though why, and in what ten-minute period, she couldn't begin to guess.

"He . . . didn't say anything to me," she said. "I didn't know you were coming until your secretary phoned this morning with a message for you to call her sometime today."

Don smiled, and her stomach did a flip-flop. "I'm sure your father meant to tell you," he said kindly, as if to a child. "It probably just slipped his mind."

Tracy was absolutely sure of it.

"I even wrote a week or so ago to confirm, though I didn't hear back from him," he continued. "I hadn't expected to, unless there was a problem." His frown returned. "Could he have forgotten I was coming?"

Tracy managed a cool shrug. "I suppose that's possible if, as you say, it's been several months since you arranged your visit. And if your letter of confirmation arrived only recently, he won't have seen it. I'm holding all his correspondence until he returns."

"I see." His brows drew together over his nose. His mouth compressed. "I take it that might not be today?"

She laughed. "Heavens, no," she said, and launched into the story she and Edie had concocted as they rapidly packed bags for the escape. "He may not be back for weeks. You know how it is. He's out following a transient pod in Alaska."

"Alaska?" Don echoed. "Then why are *you* here?"

"Me?" She affected an innocent attitude. "I just decided to stay home this summer."

"Are you still teaching at Islands West?"

She nodded, surprised that he knew so much about her life. "Winters, I teach. I spend them longing for summer so I can come home. I'd rather work with whales than teach unappreciative college students about clams and tube worms."

He chuckled. He, too, she knew, had taught marine biology.

"Unfortunately," she went on, "the whales aren't cooperating so far this summer, so it seems your trip is destined to be fruitless in more ways than one."

"I—" He paused, wondering how much to tell her. "I had really counted on seeing your father, Tracy." Merely saying that might be hint enough that a grant was in the offing, but it couldn't be helped. She'd know officially anyway as soon as he'd spoken to the professor. "Is there some way you could get in touch with him so I could arrange a place to meet him?"

She blinked for a moment, then said, "Why, no. There's no way at all for me to reach him."

Don didn't buy it. The professor he had known wouldn't leave without providing his loved ones means of reaching him any more than Don would. "But surely he'll be calling you at regular intervals?"

She smiled. "No. At least, I doubt it, but if he does, of course I'll tell him you were here, and possibly we can make some kind of . . . arrangements."

Don stared at her bland expression. Dammit, she was stonewalling him! She didn't want him to see the professor.

If he told her why he was there, would she suddenly remember a way to reach her father? He seriously considered doing just that, but as her lashes flicked down and then up again, his breath caught in his throat. As a teenager, she'd just been learning how to use them and had all too often practiced on him, flirting unmercifully. Of course, she wasn't doing so now. She likely fluttered them that way unconsciously, but the effect was as deadly.

What he should do was turn around and run, come back when her father was home, and hopefully after she'd returned to her post at the university. But then she said, "Anyway, do come on up to the house for a little while. I'm sure you'll enjoy looking around, revisiting old haunts." Deliberately, she failed to see him glance back at the overnight bag sitting in plain sight on the seat.

"I understand congratulations are in order," she went on, leading the way. "Your appointment to the board of the Meteor Foundation is a big step up in your career."

He must have made a sensible reply to her statement, because she continued a conversation he was only half aware of, even while participating in it. Following Tracy Maxwell, watching her in motion, was a pleasure he was glad he hadn't missed, as he would have if he'd stepped back into his boat and left. Her hair hung in a thick braid down her back. His fingers itched to undo it, set the gleaming brown strands free. He wondered if it would still smell the same.

He clenched his fists, determined not to submit to the strong surges of desire she elicited in him without even trying. Not until he had figured out if his own response was something to be relied on or simply an echo from the past.

She'd worn a short-sleeve thigh-length satin nightshirt when she'd come to him that time, hoping to seduce or be seduced. Her hair had been loose and flowing, curling over her shoulders, so dark as to be almost black, delicately perfumed. With her flirtatious eyes she'd beguiled him. With her soft, delicate hands she'd touched him. With her light, sweet, breathless laughter she'd almost bewitched him.

When he'd told her to go away and grow up, her eyes had gone fiery with determination. He nearly groaned, remembering how her body had felt against his when she'd flung herself into his arms, laughing at his whispered, frantic protests. Then, after he'd kissed her and set her from him, her eyes had been deep pools of mystery and confusion, but moody with newly aroused desire.

Now, following her, he found himself wanting to place his hands around her waist to see if it was as supple and firm as memory made it. He tried to see if she wore a ring on her left hand, but she stepped aside as she reached the top of the ramp and waited for him to come up beside her on the path. He swung into step beside her, looking down into her vibrant face and bright, intelligent eyes as she asked about his trip.

Those eyes didn't look moody now, or fiery, or even flirtatious. They were the eyes of a woman who knew who she was, was sure of her own place in the world—who knew what she wanted and meant to have it.

Though he tried to repress it, a new thrum of sexual excitement coursed through him. What would it be like if *he* were one of the things she meant to have, even after all these years? Would he be able to resist her seduction now? Would he want to? Would he *have* to?

Idiot! What seduction? She wasn't dressed to tantalize, though on her, a T-shirt and jeans held a definitely sexy allure. Seduction . . . and Tracy Maxwell. He smelled a hint of perfume in the breeze, tasted desire, the memory of that long-ago night and the feel of her in his arms, against his body . . . the satin of her skin, her gown.

It was all he could do not to wrap his arms around her and pull her close, see if she felt the same. See if holding her would make him feel the same.

Oh, yes, this must be part of the midlife-crisis syndrome, lusting after a woman he didn't even know. But he could get to know her. He could get to know her mouth, to rediscover the feel of it under his; its taste, its texture. He could get to know those breasts scarcely concealed by her T-shirt—their weight, their shape, what made her nipples tense and peak. He could get to know what made her sigh, what made her cry out with pleasure and need.

He could get to know the long, slender thighs, how they'd feel wrapped around him. He could get to know her softness, know intimately the way it would welcome his hardness, the way it would ripple around him in tight, hot spasms as she reached a—

"Where would you like to start?" she asked.

TWO

"*Start?*"

She met his gaze, blinking in surprise at his tone. "On your tour down memory lane," she explained. "Would you prefer to come inside and see what we've done to the office, or would you rather walk around outside first? I hope you can stay for lunch."

Don nodded as if he'd known all along what she was talking about. "I . . . uh, outside, I think, to start, but the office and lunch would be welcome later."

He chose that option because until he got used to being near her, he thought wider horizons would make it easier to keep his focus from tightening—to say nothing of certain portions of his anatomy. Yet he couldn't wait for lunch. To sit and share a meal with Tracy . . . one she had prepared . . . did she cook? Of course she cooked! She was over thirty, would be thirty-one in just a couple of months. She probably did all the things that most women did—and did them better.

That thought dried his mouth.

He walked by her side along rugged, unchanged paths. Shells crunched underfoot, crisp, sunburned moss crumbled on warm black rocks where he stepped. Salt tang and evergreen scent combined with the odor of sun-warmed creosote to transport Don back fifteen years in as many seconds.

Conversation was fractured, interspersed by long silences while she let him absorb and remember without interference.

They descended a terraced stack of shale folded by glaciers into overlapping pillows that dropped toward the high-tide mark. Here, on the very tip of Griffith Point, the wind blew strongly, and Don stopped halfway down as Tracy continued to the bottom.

He stood, captivated by the picture she made with salt spray misting her skin, the wind pressing her T-shirt to her body, combing loose wisps from her braid and fluttering them across her face as she turned to look up at him.

"Coming?" she called. She brushed the strands back and licked her lips as if to taste the salty tang, and his body responded. Quickly, needing action, he bounded down the stacked rocks to her side.

She moved apart from him, answering the question he hadn't yet asked. She answered it with the excited glimmer of her eyes, with the visible pulse in her throat, with the goose bumps prickling her upper arms, and the rapid rise and fall of her breasts. For an endless moment their glances meshed, as memory swamped Don, as he knew it swamped her.

"I remember," he said into the wind-filled silence, "all of us standing here the day I arrived, when a pod of whales came down Blackfish Sound. It was the first time I'd ever seen so much massed power."

She nodded and looked away with a smile he thought of as wistful. He wondered what it was that she remembered most about that day—and the ones that followed.

For him, the memory of that first day was sharp and clear, and what he recalled most vividly was the sobering dash of mortification he'd experienced, reference one Tracy Maxwell.

He had been there less than an hour when the shout went up, "Blackfish!"

The entire complement of the station had rushed to this very point of land, cheering as the whales came closer, counting them off, welcoming them back under a drizzly gray sky. The miserable May weather had in no way dampened the spirits of the human group, and Don had felt almost as if the whales had honored him with a personal welcome.

He'd found it difficult, though, to choose between watching the whales and looking at the professor's daughter. Her face had glowed, her round breasts heaved as she panted after the race from the house to the tip of the point. The misty rain had pearled in her dark curls. Don had forgotten for several moments that he was there to observe the whales. It wasn't until the sight of a baby orca had encouraged her to leap up and down, squealing with glee, that he'd known the score.

The professor had aimed an amused smile at his new assistant. "Kids," he'd murmured. "You'd think she was the same age as her sister instead of almost sixteen."

Sixteen? That was the first moment, filled with sick disappointment, when Don had realized he'd better keep his mind and eyes off the dark-haired girl and firmly on the whales.

There were no whales now, though, on which to fix his focus. Don glanced again at Tracy, who had lowered herself to the edge of the bottommost rock, and sat dangling her feet over its sheer side, gazing out over the blue expanse of water to where a bald eagle dipped out of the sky and skimmed the surface. It struggled to rise, a silvery fish clutched in its talons, huge, powerful wings beating.

As he had all those years before, Don was hard put to choose between the woman and the wildlife. As he sat beside her, she planted her hands several inches behind her hips, leaned back, and tilted her face up, tracking the flight of the eagle.

His gaze clung to the curve of her throat, the delicate line of her jaw, the shell-like perfection of an ear tinged pink by the brisk wind. Then, as the eagle went out of sight behind the tall trees that crowned the island, Tracy's gaze meshed with his.

She smiled.

He smiled back.

For Tracy, it was a timeless moment filled with

crashing waves, rich sea scents . . . and Don. She held his gaze, trying to read it, but it was softly enigmatic, sheltering mysteries she couldn't solve, depths she couldn't plumb, and questions she couldn't answer. She felt poised, not only on a cliff above a raging sea, but on the brink of something big, overpowering, and somehow threatening. She had to look away from him, back out to sea, scanning, always scanning, for a telltale plume of steam, for the glint of black dorsal silvered by water and sun.

Whales. Her reason for living. She'd do well to concentrate on them and forget the man beside her.

Oh, sure! The man beside her was unforgettable. Time had proven that beyond a shadow of a doubt.

Though she didn't look at him, she was supremely aware of the breadth of Don's shoulders, the power of his thighs, the left one not quite touching hers. He breathed deeply and leaned back, his arms and torso forming a tripod as he tilted his head, closing his eyes.

In a day he had come from about the thirty-third parallel of latitude, to midway between the fiftieth and fifty-first. She wondered if the northern sun felt thin on his face, if he was missing his San Diego home, his family. She wondered, too, at the strength of the attraction they shared, and if it truly was shared. If it was, why wasn't he running? The Don she'd known before would be.

Quietly, she rose to her feet and stole away, needing to be apart from him. She sat on a rock well above him and just looked, enjoying the view, wishing it didn't feel so right, didn't impart such . . . satisfaction, seeing him as part of the scene before her. It was foolish and futile and so much beneath her to dream even secret dreams about a man she knew she couldn't have, about a *life* she knew she couldn't have, that she couldn't believe she was doing it.

Yet from the minute she'd known Don Jacobs was on his way there, she'd been thinking about him in a special way, even while telling herself she'd use their mutual attraction—if it still existed—only as a means to an end.

She remembered her conversation with Edie that morning right after the phone call.

"Vamp him?" Edie had echoed Tracy's laughing description of what she'd do to get rid of Don Jacobs. "What does that mean?"

Tracy had tossed her head so her hair fell over one eye and struck a pose. "It means, my dear, innocent little sister, that I'll come on to the man so strong, his eyes will cross, his knees will buckle, and he'll run away to safety, just the way he did last time." She slinked across Edie's bedroom with a gauzy scarf draped half over her face and down her front, humming "The Stripper."

"What do you mean, the last time? The last time we saw him, we were kids, and he didn't run away. He left because he and Dad disagreed."

Tracy flipped her hair off her face. Her grin replaced by a sober look, she fixed her sister with a steady gaze. "*You* were a kid that summer. I was damn near a woman. I wanted to be a woman."

She hesitated, then told her sister something she

had never volunteered to another living soul. "I wanted Don Jacobs to make me a woman. I . . . threw myself at him. That's why he left so abruptly. Sure, maybe he didn't agree entirely with Dad's approach to orca studies, but that wasn't his real reason for leaving. I kissed him, Edie, and despite himself, he kissed me back."

She closed her eyes for a second. "And *how* he kissed me back! Then left the very next morning as if the hounds of hell were after him. So I know he'll do it again."

Edie stared at her as she plopped onto the edge of the bed. "If I was ten, you were fifteen years old! Of course he ran! Trace, he had to have been thirty or so! What man in his right mind would want a fifteen-year-old kid?"

Tracy leaned her fists on the dresser and gazed at her sister's reflection in the mirror. "He'd just turned twenty-six when he arrived. I celebrated my sixteenth birthday two months later. But I felt twenty-five, looked twenty-one, and knew it. And he wanted me. Believe me. He wanted me bad. I'd been teasing him for months."

She swallowed hard, dropped her head, and squeezed her eyes shut.

Though she'd sought it, she hadn't known exactly what it was she'd wanted. What she got was nothing like the eager and awkward fumblings she'd exchanged at parties with boys her own age. Don Jacobs was a *man*, and while she'd known that, she wasn't fully prepared for the potency of the feelings she'd unleashed in herself as well as in him. The evidence of his desire for her had frightened her even while it thrilled her, producing a heady sense of power that had been at confusing odds with the accompanying weakness in her limbs. It was something she'd never forgotten any more than she'd forgotten his scathing anger, his blistering indictment of her actions—and his. Nor had she ever forgotten his firm rejection, not only of her, but of his own response.

"Oh, yes," she said more to herself than to her sister. "He wanted me." She looked up. "Dad and I saw him six years ago in San Diego when we went down for a conference there. He wanted me then, and walked away from it. So I know that all I have to do is come on to him again, and he'll vamoose."

"You're crazy!" Edie's blue eyes went wide. "What if he *doesn't* run? Then we'll be in worse trouble, because if he reacts like every other man does to you, he'll want to settle right in. Trace, use your head," she implored. "He can't run if his knees are buckled. Throw yourself at him and you'll stick—and *we'll* be stuck with *him*."

"He'll run. Trust me. I know Donald Jacobs."

"Why will he? You're not sixteen now. Age is no impediment."

Tracy stood erect and turned. "Maybe not, but there is an impediment. He got married not six weeks after he left here."

"And you've never forgiven him for that?"

Edie's narrow-eyed gaze and probing question startled Tracy. "What?" she hooted with laughter.

"Of course I have! Good heavens, as you said, I was a kid. That summer was nearly half my lifetime ago."

Her innate honesty, though, forced her to admit, if only to herself, that she had been devastated by his marrying so quickly after leaving Blackfish Island. His marriage had rendered invalid several wonderful, graphic fantasies involving him on his knees, apologizing and groveling, begging for a second chance, while she made him suffer—briefly but intensely.

"What worries me is what if for half your life, consciously or unconsciously, you've dreamed of trying it with him again," Edie said. "I do remember him, you know, and he was very good-looking. And really nice, too, if I recall it right."

"Yes, he was both. He wasn't the kind of guy who'd tangle with a teenager, and he's not now the kind of man to cheat on his wife. That's why he turned away from me so quickly in San Diego. So I'll flirt with him a little, subtly remind him of the way he responded to me that summer, when he must have been engaged to be married. I'll tell him what a thrill it was to see him again in San Diego, and how I wished we could have spent some time together." That would be easy to say. It was true. She had wished for it.

"Then," Tracy continued with a grin that failed to elicit a smile from her sister, "I'll mention his wife—the way Dad did in San Diego—and watch him ride out of here on a magic carpet of guilt."

"Good luck." Edie's tone was bitter. "If you believe marriage has ever been an obstacle to a man's taking what he wants—especially if it's offered—you're in trouble."

Now, sitting on a slab of shale thirty yards or so from Don Jacobs, who seemed content to commune with the sea, Tracy knew her sister was right. She was in trouble for sure, but not for the reasons Edie had feared. It wasn't Don Jacobs who was in danger of succumbing. No, not Don Jacobs at all. And for that very reason, her notion that she could get rid of him by "vamping" him needed some serious revision.

Yet he still had to go.

Presently, Don realized that Tracy wasn't at his side any longer, though for how long she'd been gone he couldn't have said. He'd kept his eyes closed, kept his breathing steady and even, and simply reveled in her nearness, enjoyed knowing that at any second he could open his eyes, turn his head, and see her profile. That if he chose, he could speak, and she would respond in her husky bedroom voice, gaze at him through her thick, luxurious lashes. He pretended to himself that when he did open his eyes, he'd have the right to lean toward her and touch his mouth to hers, to part her plump, ripe lips and taste her.

When he did open his eyes and found her gone, he was disoriented for several seconds, to the point of wondering if he'd dreamed the entire trip. But no. The air was sharply cool compared to what he was used to, and so clear, he could pick out individual trees on Hansen Island, slightly over a mile away.

A pebble hit the rock beside him, and he turned to

look behind. He saw her then, a hundred feet above him.

She sat on a black fold of shale, a bank of bright yellow Scotch broom behind her, a circle of dark green trees forming a backdrop below the blue sky and cotton-candy clouds. She picked up another pebble and bounced it down the rocks toward him, then stood and waved. She was on her feet waiting as he loped up the stacked stone slabs to her, laughing.

He tugged her braid. "Throw rocks at me, will you?"

"Anything to get your attention."

You've got that, lady, he didn't say, but knew she knew it all the same.

They shared another smile, then walked on. From the island's summit, through a gap in the stately cedars, he saw a pair of kayakers crossing between two islands, playing with the waves. He smiled, recalling himself and Tracy and several students in similar little craft bobbing across the sound to commingle with the whales. That was the memory his one snapshot of her had preserved.

Tracy, with sparkling delight in her eyes as she paddled beside him, while orcas swam all around them. Tracy, aglow with summer and sweet youth and the magic of self-discovery, with a juvenile whale spy-hopping in the background. The whale was supposed to have been the subject of his camera's lens, but cameras don't lie. His focus had been firmly on the girl.

"Remember this?" Tracy asked after they'd descended the zigzag path back to the level of the house.

The sound of her voice, the feel of her hand on his elbow, brought him out of his musings.

"The bonsai forest!" he said as he blinked and realized they'd entered a sheltered garden. It was bounded on two sides by the curve of a rock bluff, and the third by a moss-topped six-foot-high stone wall that blocked the ocean winds. A back wall of the house sheltered the other side. "You know, I'd forgotten about your mother's hobby."

"It's mine now," she said softly.

"Of course. I'm sorry," he said. "I should have offered my condolences earlier. Forgive me."

"It's all right. I wasn't sure you'd have heard anyway. But thank you."

"I liked and respected your mother," Don said. "She was good to me that summer I spent here. Her death must have been a terrible blow to your father. She was so young to die." He thought the professor must have had at least twenty years on his wife. He'd likely expected to predecease her by a long time.

"Yes." Tracy nodded. "She'd be fifty-five now. I still miss her terribly."

As she bent her head, Don gave in to the impulse to touch her nape, feeling wisps of hair brush the back of his hand. "I'm so sorry, Tracy. I know that doesn't help much, but I am." Though both his parents were living and healthy, he could empathize.

Tracy nodded, as much to shrug off Don's light touch before it burned her skin as in acknowledgment. "Thank you," she murmured again. She crouched and carefully repositioned a branch on a miniaturized azalea, bending it, with its supporting coil of wire, another quarter inch toward the direction she wanted it to take. She sighed and lifted the potted shrub onto a long, narrow table, brushing a hammock of spiderwebs from between two of its branches.

"How's your little sister?" he asked. "I don't remember her name. What's she doing now?"

"Edie." She hadn't really required a reminder of her plan to dispatch this man, and the reason for it, but his question certainly provided one. "She's away with Dad."

"Why her and not you? You're the one who's worked most closely with him all these years, aren't you?"

She shrugged negligently. "We all work together, more or less. Somebody had to stay here and man the machinery this year, and why shouldn't it be me?"

"Because you . . ." He let it trail off; it really wasn't his business. But he couldn't help wondering if she and her father had had some kind of falling out. He wished she'd talk to him, wanted to break through this invisible shell of reserve that he realized now surrounded her, keeping her emotionally apart from him regardless of how gracious a guide and hostess she was.

The past stood between them like a locked gate. Maybe if he could get over that hurdle, a way would open up for them to travel beyond the old memories and start making new ones.

Tracy glanced at him, wondering at the thoughts that imparted such a brooding intensity to his eyes.

Then, as if becoming aware of her scrutiny, he shook his head and grinned. "I can't say I blame you for staying here and letting the whales come to you. It's got to be more comfortable doing your research right in your own front yard than from the pitching deck of a ship."

"It is," she agreed, and would have moved on, but he caught her hand, holding her by his side.

"I remember your delight in the orcas that summer, how you personalized them, even to the point of naming them and their offspring, rather than sticking with the letter-number system used by other researchers."

She shrugged and looked down. She'd really prefer not to discuss that summer. She detected in him none of the guilt she thought would inhibit him, none of the shame she herself had suffered in weak moments ever since.

"I was a giddy kid that summer." She tugged gently in a vain attempt to free her hand. "Scientific experiments held little charm for me."

"I remember," Don said, his eyes becoming hooded as he touched her cheek with one fingertip, the light caress bringing her face up so their gazes met. "I remember a lot about that summer. And one 'experiment' you *were* willing to try."

Tracy drew a deep breath and let it out slowly, silently. "So we finally get to it." She wasn't aware she'd spoken aloud until Don replied.

"Did you think we wouldn't?" he asked. "It's

something we've both been remembering ever since I stepped onto the float."

Somehow, she conjured up a light laugh. "But maybe we remember it differently, put greater emphasis on different . . . aspects of it." She twisted her hand free. "Shall we compare notes over lunch?"

Don wrapped his hands over her shoulders, holding her in place as she would have turned and walked away. She couldn't speak, could only stand there and stare into his intense blue eyes, listening to the *ting! ting! ting!* of Con's hammer on something metal in the machine shop not far away.

"I'm not ready for lunch," he said. "Let's walk on and talk instead." He dropped his hands from her shoulders, leaving two suddenly cold patches on her skin.

"All right." She forced herself to go on meeting his probing gaze, keeping her own open and candid as she stepped away a foot or two. "What, specifically, do you want to talk about?"

She saw his mouth tighten. "Don't play games, Tracy," he said. "You're not a child now. Maybe . . . maybe that's why I'm finding this even more difficult than I anticipated."

She realized he'd read the question in her eyes when he added impatiently, "Apologizing, Tracy." His voice dropped into its lowest registers, his gaze was somber. "I wanted to do it at that conference six years ago, when you came to San Diego. But with your father sitting at the same table, I couldn't."

His Adam's apple bobbed as he swallowed. "I, uh,

called your room the next day, thinking maybe we could get together for coffee or something, but you'd already checked out. So let me say it now. I do apologize for my actions. What I did, and what I said, my trying to put the blame on you, was wrong, and I've regretted it ever since."

His sincerity touched her more deeply than she wanted him to know. She hoped her laugh hid her surprise and the surge of emotions his words aroused. She took a few more steps away. He followed. "There's no need to apologize, Don," she said, her voice too high, too thin. "Not for a simple little kiss."

"That was no simple little kiss. You came to me, all innocent and eager and certain I would welcome you. I've thought many times I must somehow have given you reason to believe that, and then I—" He broke off, his face looking suddenly older. "I hurt you."

She shrugged to show how little importance an event fifteen years in the past held for her. "You hurt only my feelings. You sent me away with a bug in my ear, exactly as you should have. So what?"

"I sent you away with more than a bug in your ear. I was pretty, um . . ."

"Hard on me?" Tracy provided with another laugh. Her deliberate innuendo was rewarded by a dark flush staining the taut skin over his cheekbones.

The color enhanced the blue of his eyes, imparting depth and mystery, and revealing a hint of anger that sent a ripple of something potent and exciting through her. "Oh, you certainly were that, but never mind. Apology accepted, though it wasn't required. I hope you'll accept mine too." She spun away and made her escape.

"Tracy . . ." His voice was rough, and she nearly turned back, but the instinct of self-preservation kept her in motion. She strode along a winding path through the bonsai forest, past miniaturized trees and shrubs, some in pots, others in small natural pockets in the basalt structure of the bluff, feeling as if her roots and development were as constricted as that of the plants. She longed for wings, yearned to fly, or for fins and the ability to dive deep and swim far. She wanted space, distance from all the troublesome aspects of her life—including this newly introduced one.

Above all, she did not want to rehash that summer.

Don stood for a second, staring at her swaying hips, her long, enticing legs. She was running away, fleeing from him. Or from herself?

Did she run because she, too, felt there was a chapter or two of unfinished business between them? Did the thought of opening those pages scare and excite her as much as it did him?

He followed. "I think we need to talk about that incident," he said when he caught up to her.

"Why?" She met his gaze defiantly. "It's over. You apologized. I apologized. There's nothing more to discuss."

"I don't agree. I have things to say about it, if you don't. Will you give me the opportunity to do that?" He hadn't the vaguest idea of what more he might say about it, but it was the only reason he could think of for prolonging their discussion.

"All right," she agreed, sitting on a shaded bench under a thick-limbed hemlock tree and patting the green-painted slats beside her. "If you insist. I'm sure we have time to do that before you rush away to catch your ferry."

Don lowered himself onto the bench, laying one arm across the back of it. He breathed in the scent of evergreens, the earthiness of moss, the bite of salt air, and the softer, lighter scent he recognized as definitely being Tracy's. He fastened one fist around her braid and tugged gently, bringing her face up toward his.

"Now, what," he asked softly, "gave you the impression that I have a ferry to catch?"

THREE

Tracy hid her uneasiness behind her lashes. None of this was part of her plan! She needed to regain control —assuming she'd ever had it. Slowly, deliberately, she opened her eyes wide and met Don's gaze, saw his blur and soften in some almost indefinable manner, but one she recognized as the expression of a man about to fall under a spell. That was better.

"Since Dad's not here," she said, "I didn't suppose for a minute you'd have any reason to stay."

"Didn't you?" His voice was deep, soft, and seemed to seep into all her little corners. "Maybe my seeing your father was . . . incidental to my real reason for coming here."

"Oh?" she said, concentrating on reclaiming her poise. This breathlessness of hers, the wild hammering of her heart, was more than a little disconcerting. She ran the tip of her tongue over suddenly dry lips. "And what might your real purpose be?"

"Maybe just to say hello."

"Oh," she said, going for humor. "Hello."

"*This* is the right way to say hello." He dropped his head unexpectedly and took her mouth in a kiss that sent her senses reeling, trapped her breath in her chest, and made her glad she was sitting down.

Completely unable to help herself, and without thought of consequences, she opened her mouth at his silent bidding and melted against him. He took liberties no man had ever taken before on a first kiss, and it was only dimly that she managed to recall that this was not their first kiss. It may have been their second, but neither of them had forgotten exactly how to fit their mouths together for the most devastating effect, forgotten the swift surge of desire that sprang up between them to set blood aboil.

He groaned as his arms locked around her, pulling her to the hard plane of his chest, pressing her breasts against him. She sighed as her arms slid up over his shoulders, the fingers of one hand tunneling through the satiny thickness of his hair. He stroked her face with his fingertips, slid the caress down her throat and across her shoulder.

As he massaged the ridge beside her spine, Tracy went limp, her head lolling on his shoulder, her eyes closed, her lips parted, soft sounds rising through her throat. He kissed her face, her eyelids, her cheeks, and the corners of her lips. She cried aloud and shuddered in pleasure at the sensation of his lips on her neck.

Then he stopped, dropped his head, and buried his face against her shoulder, breathing as hard as if he'd run five miles. His hands tracked restlessly over her back, molding her waist, her hips, her thighs.

But the kiss, it seemed, was over. And just in time.

She extricated herself, smiled, and leaned back, crossing her legs. "Well! Goodness," she said. "Fifteen years of marriage have certainly done wonders for your technique. Give my compliments to your wife."

Technique? Don stared at her, trying to read her eyes behind the thick curtain of lashes that shadowed her expression. If it hadn't been for the still-rapid pulse he saw in her throat, for the delicate flush rising from her neck to cover her face, he might have thought her completely unmoved by the kiss they had just shared. But he knew. And now he also knew what she'd been up to.

His apology had not been enough. This had to be punishment for a past sin.

But which sin? The one of kissing a sixteen-year-old virgin as if she were the experienced woman she wanted to be? Or the one of stopping before it was too late?

"I would," he said, "assuming I had a wife."

Her eyes went wide and her mouth went slack for an instant. "You . . . don't?"

He almost laughed at the consternation flooding her face. It would have been a more appropriate expression if, after kissing her the way he had, he'd suddenly announced that he did have one.

"But you—" She broke off, closed her eyes for a second, then opened them as she opened the fists she had clenched in her lap.

He watched her collect her scattered thoughts, bring herself under full control, and admired the swift way she accomplished it. She squared her shoulders, thrust out her chin, and got to her feet, stuffing her hands into the back pockets of her jeans. "Then my compliments to . . . to you," she said. "I'll see about hurrying lunch along so you can eat before you leave."

She spun on one heel and strode toward the back door of the house, leaving Don to stare after her.

Tracy shut the door behind her very, very carefully, aware of the simmering pressure within her, afraid to move too suddenly, lest it erupt.

Edie had been right. Many factors had changed: Don was no longer married. He wasn't about to be scared off. And she appeared to have lost all control of her own body, even her emotions, which kept telling her to go back for more. Dammit, she was crazy. It was wrong to want more.

Yet, another part of her argued, how could it be wrong, when it felt so right? She had wanted that kiss as much as she'd wanted the one she'd gotten fifteen years earlier, and again she'd wanted it to go on until she'd eked out every bit of sensuous pleasure she could derive from physical contact with him.

If her body had had its way, she knew exactly where a kiss like that would have led, and she'd have been powerless to stop it. She wouldn't have wanted to stop it. She had never wanted to make love with a man the way she wanted it with Don Jacobs.

It was far, far more, she knew, than a mere hangover from the past. She wanted the man he was now.

Even knowing nothing about him beyond the fact that if he knew of her father's illness, he could inadvertently destroy everything she had worked for—she still wanted him.

But that was the physical side of it. What about the emotional aspect of what was happening? What about trust? Could she give it? What about commitment? Could she accept the physical release she knew he could give her without feeling fully committed to him, without knowing where his true commitments might lie?

She drew herself up short. It was far too soon to allow her hormones to sweep her into a physical relationship, and it was also far too early to think about such serious issues as emotional commitment. What she needed to do was step back, put some space between them, and keep it there while she thought this through.

Because whatever else happened, she had to protect her father from the public having the least hint that all was not well with his mind.

That's what she had to do, what she had to concentrate on, what she had to remember.

Maybe . . . in time, she could seek a life of her own, but right now her life was dedicated to protecting her father, finishing his studies, and getting them published under his name.

Before it had to be done posthumously.

She had no time for anything else.

She whirled to face the door when Don opened it, following her in. To her chagrin, instead of standing her ground, she discovered too late that she had fled to the middle of the kitchen and found there was no place to run. She came to a swift halt and stood staring at him.

Don read her startled expression and smiled. "Did you hope I had gone?" he asked, then chuckled at her obvious disgruntlement.

"Sorry," he went on, not at all apologetically. "I hadn't planned on going anywhere in any kind of hurry." He paced toward her. She took two steps back, only to be stopped by the bulk of the refrigerator.

He planted his hands on either side of her head, leaning toward her, not touching but close. He lifted one hand from the cool, smooth surface of the refrigerator door, slid it under her chin, and tilted her face up, delighted by the contrast, by the warm, smooth surface of her skin.

As if the pulse under his hand weren't hammering at ninety miles an hour, as if those two patches of bright color weren't making little flags on her cheekbones, as if her breathing weren't as shallow and rapid as his, she spoke casually. "You can use the phone here," she said, indicating the one on the counter, "or in there to call your secretary." She gestured toward the office-cum-workshop, across the hall from the kitchen.

"Maybe I won't call just yet," he said.

"As you like. But she did sound as if there was a degree of . . . urgency."

He dipped his head closer. "I don't think she knows the meaning of the term." He brushed his mouth across hers, feeling her lips quiver slightly. "But I do," he added. Her eyes went dark and moody through her lashes. He smiled. "And I think maybe you do too."

He kissed her the same light way again, feeling that pulse increase to about one-sixty, comparable with his.

She brought one hand up between them and placed it on his chest, but before he could learn if she meant to shove him away, the door behind him swung open and banged against its stopper.

"Well!" boomed a voice he remembered instantly. "You don't waste any time, do you, Jacobs?"

He wheeled, feeling as guilty as he would have if anyone had come upon him kissing Tracy fifteen years before.

"Connie!" he said, staring at the old woman in the doorway. "For the love of Mike! I never expected you to still be here."

Con marched over to him, massive hands on overalled hips, and gave him a long, intent once-over. "Seeing as you were trying to get to the fridge through young Tracy, I suppose you plan to eat us out of house and home again."

"Sure, if I get the chance." He flicked a glance at Tracy, who still stood backed against the refrigerator. "My appetite's fully whetted," he added just before transferring his gaze back to Con.

"I take it you're still chief cook and mechanic?" He sniffed the aroma of the pot of soup simmering on the stove.

She nodded curtly.

"It's good to see you again, Connie," he said. "I've never had hotcakes that could measure up to yours."

"Hmmph!" Con snorted. "Don't bother soft-soapin' me. It won't buy you nothin'. An' don't call me that sissy name."

He grinned. "You know, I *used* to be scared of you, Con."

"Stay that way, sonny."

He laughed and swept her into a bear hug. "It's a long time since anybody's called me 'sonny.' "

Again, Con said, "Hmmph," but her gaze was soft as she shrugged his arms off her. "It's even longer since any young buck's given me a hug."

Tracy left the two of them grinning at each other and slipped away to the office. It took several minutes to get her pulse and respiration back to normal. Even listening to his laughter, the rumble of his voice, disturbed her. She should have paid attention to her sister. His lack of a wife, lack of the impediment she'd been counting on, made everything different, that much more risky.

She frowned. There need be no risk. He was leaving after lunch.

"Thanks, Con," he said, and she realized he had crossed the hall and was speaking to Con from the office doorway. "I appreciate it."

"Appreciate what?" Tracy asked as he came in.

"She's going to make up the bed for me in my old cabin."

Damn! So much for whatever hopes she might

have entertained of enlisting Con's help in getting rid of Don Jacobs anytime soon. All right, so it was up to her. She gazed at him, into those blue, blue eyes, feeling her good sense spiral away like water down a drain. *Do it!* Tracy told herself. *Do it now. Tell him he can't stay.* All she had to do was tell him she didn't find it convenient to have a house guest. He was a well-bred man. He'd understand and bow out gracefully. Anybody would.

Instead, she opened her mouth and said, "It hasn't been occupied for at least three years. It'll need to be aired out too."

"I'm sure Con will take care of it." Tracy saw his gaze sweep around the workroom she had long shared with her father—a work area he had once shared with Professor Maxwell. Obviously, he'd see many changes.

"I'm surprised to see regular telephones here," he said. "Before, it was just the radiophone."

She turned and sidled away from the heat that emanated from his body, putting several yards between them. "Edie writes a good grant. She got us one from the federal government for improving the facilities a few years back. Part of it went to run phone and electric cables underwater from Malcolm Island."

She pulled the chair out from her desk and, holding on to its back, rolled it back and forth on its casters. "It makes it possible for us to have a fax machine, and a much more sophisticated computer system. We really needed that."

Don nodded and came to her, perching one hip on her desk. He'd shed the light Windbreaker he'd been wearing. The short sleeves of his blue polo shirt revealed muscular forearms, liberally sprinkled with sun-bleached golden hair, through which a dark tan showed. Aware she was staring, she looked down and gestured at the phone on her desk. "Go ahead and make your call," she said, then glanced back up at him with a smile. "I'll give Con a hand with lunch."

She heard his swift intake of breath, and before she could move, his hand slid under her braid, and he cupped the back of her neck and tilted her face to his. He took her lips in a kiss that melted her knees and made her sway against him. Moments later, he lifted his head, steadied her, and smiled ruefully into her eyes.

"I wish you wouldn't keep doing that," he said, and she gave a laugh of surprise.

"Doing what? I didn't do anything. *You* did."

"It's the way you look at me," he said. "With your eyes all big and dark and moody one second, then shy and hiding behind those lashes of yours. Flirting, beguiling me, tempting me."

"I . . . wasn't," she protested, but he only laughed and withdrew his hand from under her hair, letting his fingers trail slowly across her shoulder, down her arm, and off the tips of her fingers until the contact was broken.

They stood in silence, staring at each other.

Con called then that lunch was ready. Tracy surprised Don by holding her hand out to him. "Coming?" she said. "I'm sure you're as hungry as I am."

He caught her fingers, her gaze, and held both. "Probably more," he said.

For a moment she looked into his eyes, then demurely lowered her lashes, slipped her fingers out of his, and turned. But not before he saw a hint of a smile curve her lips. Did she really murmur, "Don't be too sure . . ."

Before he could ask her to repeat what she'd said, she was gone. As before, he followed her willingly. It was much, much later when he remembered he'd never called his office.

"Good soup, Con," Tracy said, though she could scarcely taste it for remembering how Don's kisses had tasted. Somehow, she had to keep herself from dwelling on that. That wasn't how it was supposed to be. Somehow, she had to try to keep up a reasonable conversation, or Con would start making pointed comments.

"Of course it's good soup." Con sniffed. "Have I ever made another kind?"

"As a matter of fact, there was that cod chowder you tried to get us to eat once," Tracy said. "Now, that," she continued, addressing Don, "was truly gruesome." She went on to describe it in detail, wrinkling her nose, pulling disgusted faces, and fending off Con's acerbic comments about ungrateful children and threats about taking up the offer of a local logging camp in search of a cook/handyman.

Finally, with a snort, Con shoved her chair back

and stood, interrupting one of Don's more lurid descriptions of some of the meals he had cooked for himself and his son after his divorce. "If you kids want to sit here all afternoon and swap horror stories about food, you go ahead. I've got better things to do."

She plopped plates of warm, aromatic gingerbread cake slathered with whipped cream in front of both of Tracy and Don. "The Johnson one-eighty is up and running again," she said. "I put it on the red Zodiac, so you can roll it out of the shed as soon as you've finished the dishes. You," she continued, pointing a finger at Don, "can give her a hand."

With a glance at Tracy, she said, "I told him he could stay the night."

Tracy stared pointedly into Con's eyes. She nodded because there was little else she could do at the moment. "Tonight'll be fine, but then, unless the whales show up, I'm off to Campbell River for the weekend." For the first time in her life she was going to pray for an absence of whales. Turning to Don, she added, "I hope you'll forgive me, but this really isn't a good time for you to have come."

Before Don could reply, Con said, "I'll take over some stuff for your breakfasts, in case you wake up early like you used to." She set a pound of coffee and a bag of sugar into a basket, and reached into the fridge for eggs.

Breakfasts? Plural? All at once Tracy realized Con intended to make Don very, very comfortable in that cabin, as if she wanted him to settle right in and stay.

The woman was nuts! But then, she'd always been a law unto herself, unless curbed.

"Con, there are plenty of empty beds in the house, and for only one ni—" she began, but Con gave one of her most ferocious snorts.

"Hah! Do you think for a minute I'm gonna let you spend the night in this house with a man and no chaperon?" Then, as if it had been Don who'd made the comment about empty beds, she wheeled on him and glared. "Not this side of my grave, sonny! Got it?"

"Got it," he said, sitting straighter.

"Good. And when I've got your cottage ready, I'm going home to take my nap, so you kids keep the racket down." She turned to stomp away before Tracy could remind her that she wore two hearing aids she had only to turn off when she didn't want to be disturbed.

"Hey, not so fast," Don said, catching Con's hand as she went past and dragging her down into his lap. She gave a squawk of surprise mingled with mock anger, but he shut her up with a smacking kiss on her cheek. "Thanks, Connie," he continued. "That was a great lunch. What do you do, keep notes on the favorite desserts of all the different men you meet?"

"I never met a man who didn't like gingerbread and whipped cream," she said gruffly. "Now, you let me go, you big, goofy boy! I'm too old and fat to sit on a man's knee."

"Baloney," he said. "You're just a nice, plump armful."

He kissed her again, just as loudly and on the lips, and let her go. To Tracy's amusement, Con was blushing furiously.

"Don't laugh," Con said, rounding on her. "You'll just encourage him."

"Yes, ma'am." Tracy said, grinning in spite of herself. "I wasn't laughing. Honest. I don't believe in encouraging big, goofy boys any more than you do. No way. Not me."

Con gave her a mock cuff on the side of her head and stomped away, but Tracy knew she was delighted with Don's attention. All right, then. Con didn't ask for a lot, and this was her home too. If she wanted Don to spend the night, then he could spend the night. Besides, Edie couldn't possibly bring Dad back that day. He'd need at least one night's rest. And so would Edie, after the trip she must have had, getting Dad to Campbell River.

"Thanks," she said when Con was out of earshot. "I'm not sure any of us show her our appreciation often enough. I think you've just made her entire month."

He chuckled. "She sure made mine. 'Big, goofy boy' indeed, and putting me in a cabin so she can lock you up in the house. She made me feel as if I were in my twenties again."

"You don't look a whole lot older than when you were here before," Tracy said, diving into her gingerbread. "So she thinks she has to treat you the same."

"But I am a whole lot older," he said with a steady stare into her eyes. "Believe me, I am." He paused for a significant moment, then added softly, "And so are you. Maybe that locked door is a good idea."

They ate in silence for a few minutes, then he glanced sideways at her. "Never married, Tracy?"

She shook her head and stood, collecting dishes as she moved toward the sink. "Came close once, but it never . . . happened." She turned on the tap, squirted dish detergent into the running water, and watched the suds build.

"So what *did* happen?" he asked, shouldering her out of the way and dropping a handful of cutlery into the water.

She shouldered him back. It was like trying to nudge a mountain aside. "You don't have to do that," she said.

"Yes, I do. Con said so." He rinsed the cutlery under the running water and dropped it into the bottom of the draining rack. "You dry and put away, since you know where things go." He had washed the last cake plate and set it in the rack before he asked, "How close did you come?"

She shrugged. There was no reason not to tell him. "About as close as you can get. I waited in the vestry of the church, all decked out in white silk and lace, for forty-five minutes before he had the courtesy or the courage or whatever to phone the minister and say he was somewhere south of Seattle and heading for parts unknown."

He turned her face toward him with a large, soapy hand. She saw compassion, caring, anger, all mingled in his eyes. "You all over the hurting?"

She wiped her chin dry with one upraised shoulder. "It was nearly ten years ago. So yes, I'm all over it."

He smiled. "Good," he said, and pulled the plug in the sink, letting the dirty water drain out. Together they watched it go, then he looked directly at her again and said softly, significantly, "So'm I."

A powerful surge of sexual need slammed through her so unexpectedly, she stumbled back from him. She hung up her tea towel, stuffed her fingers into her back pockets, and strolled outside, hoping she gave the impression of a woman in total control of her emotions. She was halfway to the boathouse before he caught up, and then he merely said, "Con's an amazingly versatile woman, isn't she? How long has she been with your family?"

Tracy smiled in gratitude. It was a whole lot easier to talk about Con than about why he'd felt he'd had to say what he did.

"Pss . . . *shew*!" Don came half awake at the first sound. Squinting into an unfamiliar, inky darkness, he heard the next drawn out, "Pss . . . *shew*!"

A third explosive, breathy sound brought him to a sitting position, and at the next, he was out of bed, reaching for the jeans he had discarded earlier. Dragging his pants on, he hopped to the window in the sitting room and thrust aside the curtains. The moon had not yet set, and in its light he saw, six . . . no, eight, ten, maybe more whales in three different groups, spouting as they made their stately way down Cormorant Channel and into Blackfish Sound. The westerly had died, and with it, the chop, leaving the surface of the channel mirror-smooth but for ripples as the whales broke its glassy, moon-silvered finish.

A thrill coursed through him, something elemental and atavistic, as if he were a prehistoric hunter whose prey was in sight. At that moment he thought he understood the old-time native whalers.

How must it have been, taking on those beasts with nothing more deadly than their frail dugout canoes and bone harpoons? In pitting themselves against such raw magnificence, they had in some way taken to themselves the massed power of the whales. Their stories and totems often depicted killer whales with reverence and respect he shared down deep in his soul.

He was eternally grateful there was no longer anyone needing to take them for food and oil. At least, not in these waters. Seeing them now gave him a swelling sense of unity with all of those who argued against whales in captivity, though he was fully aware of the many educational advantages in putting the animals on display.

His next thought was of Tracy, one of the strongest opponents of the practice. Where was she? Didn't she know the whales were there? Was she awake? He wanted to share these first moments of the pods' arrival with her.

He stuffed his bare feet into his shoes, grabbed a sweatshirt, and rushed outside. He laughed. She knew.

She was awake. Lights blazed all over the house. She'd join him any minute now. Either that, or she'd already be at the tip of Griffith Point, watching the parade.

Hauling the shirt on over his head, he ducked back into the house and grabbed his camcorder out of his bag, then trotted along a rough path until he stood on the promontory that offered the best view of the animals' approach. Tracy hadn't yet arrived, but he knew she'd be there soon. No one who cared about orcas could miss this spectacle.

Lifting the camera, he began filming, hoping the ambient moonlight would provide enough illumination. This was for his son, and he wanted every second of it on tape.

Towering dorsals sliced the waters. Great, gleaming black backs with pale saddle patches rose sleekly in long, smooth curves, and slid below the still surface with scarcely a ripple to mark their passage. With each broaching, gushes of white steam puffed upward, ribboned across the water, and drifted away in wisps of moonlit mist.

Unexpected tears stung Don's eyes, though whether at the sheer majesty of the animals, or in sorrow that he stood alone at this poignant moment, he couldn't have said.

This was what he had wanted to share with his son. *This* was what he'd wanted Eric to experience firsthand! Damn Muriel's hide! If it weren't for her overly developed compulsion to show Don exactly who held the upper hand at all times, Eric would be at his side right now. Damn her to hell for depriving them both of a shared experience he'd long promised his son.

He focused his mind, as well as his camcorder, on the whales again, determined to capture all of it for Eric.

On they came, the steady, stately progression of an ancient civilization on the move. They kept themselves in small groups. Six whales here, nine way over there on the far shore; five, or was it seven, heading into Weynston Passage, disappearing among the cluttered, dark silhouettes of Plumper Islands. Another pod broached, sounded, then failed to reappear, but he knew they would, when and where they chose.

They were not putting on a show for him. Orcas had been arriving and departing through Blackfish Sound since before there were people to erroneously dub them with the name "blackfish"; since before native peoples had launched their first dugouts; perhaps even since before man had crawled out of the ooze. These waters had belonged to the orcas since time began, and would belong to them forever.

Or at least as long as there were caring people like the Maxwells to speak out for them, to guard their passage and protect their habitat.

The professor . . . and Tracy. Where the hell was she? He could scarcely believe she had slept through the whales' return.

He frowned as he panned slowly again, thinking about a snippet of conversation he'd overheard as he'd returned to the house for dinner that evening. Tracy, he suspected, had been scolding Con for having told him he could stay.

"What the hell are you trying to do, making the man so comfortable we'll never get rid of him?" she'd been saying. Her words had frozen him in his tracks long enough to hear Con's gruff reply that she didn't see any logic in Tracy's "crazy insistence" on following an old man's dream.

"What about your dream?" Con had said.

"What about it?" Tracy's retort had been throaty, as if she were on the verge of tears. In that moment, Don couldn't have backed away, or cleared his throat, or done anything else to give away his eavesdropping. "I'm young. My dream can wait. And maybe making sure Dad's comes true will make mine easier to achieve. But I need to get on with it, not spend my time entertaining a house guest. Maybe if you'd left well enough alone, he'd be gone by now."

"Do you really want him gone?" Con asked. "Remember, girlie, I know when you're lyin'," she added.

Tracy laughed. "When it comes to Don Jacobs, I don't know what I really want."

"Right. All the more reason to let him stick around until you figure it out. And tell him the truth, Tracy. That's my advice. Tell the man the truth."

What truth? Don wondered again as the last of the nearby whales sounded.

He shut off the camera and turned back toward the house, scanning the path to see if Tracy was in sight. Again he saw nothing but the blazing lights in the windows. With a frown, he cast one last look at the whales. Now that they were there, they'd stick around for weeks, if not months. He'd see them again.

It wasn't like Tracy to miss this. Something must be wrong.

FOUR

"Con! Wake up!" For the third time, Tracy hammered on the door of Con's cottage. "Come on, Con! I need you!"

With a growl of despair, she gave up. Without her hearing aids, Con was almost impossible to rouse before nine A.M. Also, after years of cooking in logging camps filled with what she called "randy goats," she had a firmly embedded habit of never going to bed without locking all her doors and windows.

With whales blowing all around, Tracy raced homeward and flung herself at the equipment in the office. She'd have to do without Con's help.

Before she'd left to get Con, acting automatically as a result of long years of practice, she'd flipped on all the recorders. Crossing the room now, she turned down the volume on the speakers until the whales' vocalizations faded to a gentle murmur nearly lost in the background behind the different hums of active electronics.

Her adrenaline up and pumping hard, Tracy went to work checking the rolls of paper where pins busily traced the peaks and valleys of the visible manifestations of whale sounds, and attending to the different audio recorders. At each station around the room, she slipped on earphones, tracking which pod was where, making notes of time and place and probable rate of travel.

That information gave her a rough idea of when each group could be expected to reach a set position ahead on the journey and make it easier to be in place to monitor the right hydrophone at the right time.

Pods A-1 and A-3 were proceeding between Cormorant Island and Malcolm Island. Easily, she recognized the different dialects, the special clicks, beeps, and whistles passed down from mother to child among the orcas, speech patterns that shifted and changed only subtly from year to year. R pod, or possibly just a portion of it, was gliding toward her well out in Queen Charlotte Strait, to the east of Malcolm Island. It was just approaching the farthest hydrophones, distant enough that she could concentrate on closer groups for the time being.

She removed the headphones, set the recording levels as best she could, making a mental note to return and make adjustments as soon as possible.

Nothing remained static when six or eight pods were assembling to create a superpod, a relatively rare occurrence, and one that hadn't happened for three years now. She couldn't afford to miss a moment of the assembly; each was ripe with scientific data to be recorded, analyzed, and pored over at a later date. How she wished she had the staff to allow her to leave the machinery and take herself out there among the whales!

Now, when the whales were assembling, when she suspected that they were most attuned to one another, communicating greetings from pod to pod she firmly believed, was when she needed to be physically among them. She felt trapped, doing work that Edie could have handled with Con's assistance, thereby freeing Tracy and her father for their task of attempting to communicate directly with the whales.

If only . . .

She sighed. If-onlys didn't cut it. If-onlys didn't get the work done. It was Con's fault, the way she poked at her, nagging about Tracy's living her own life, fulfilling her own dream. They both knew that had been put on hold for the time being, and they both knew why.

Sometimes she wondered about Con, about where her loyalties lay. What did she want Tracy to do, abandon everything her father had ever wanted? What kind of a daughter would do that? Still, frustration ate at her, frustration she couldn't allow herself to feel. Fine, then, she'd let Con feel it for her while she did what was right.

She clenched her teeth and told herself that this, too, was important—the nuts and bolts of their research, tracking the animals, keeping a running census, trying to ascertain the health and viability of each pod in particular, and all pods in general. Okay, maybe it was being duplicated in research stations from Attu to Tierra del Fuego, but what one researcher missed, another might pick up on. Compiled and compared, the data provided a comprehensive picture of the state of North Pacific orcas.

If the population maintained a steady rate of growth, it seemed fairly safe to assume the ocean was still a healthy place to be. An unexplained drop could be the harbinger of doom, because if Earth's oceans became dangerously unhealthy for the mammals that occupied it, it could mean that Earth itself was dangerously unhealthy for the mammals that lived on the land, including mankind.

So this *was* important, and her father's particular hobbyhorse could wait until daylight.

Her own, of course, would wait a lot longer than that.

As she scurried to the next bank of recorders, she wished futilely again for not only her sister, but for a couple of students as well. Hell, what she really needed was a full crew, something they hadn't had at Blackfish Station for several years. In the meantime, though, even Con would have been better than no one.

She thought fleetingly of press-ganging the one other inhabitant of Blackfish Island, then put the idea out of her head. The fewer reasons she offered him for staying, the sooner he'd be gone.

As deliciously tempting as his kisses were, as much

as she had enjoyed his company during the day and evening, he had to leave in the morning. It was imperative, because she couldn't expect Edie and Dad to stay away for more than a day or two. Edie had likely spent her evening trying to keep Dad calm and cursing Tracy for not calling and saying it was safe to come home.

Presently, though, as she worked, listening intently to the rhythms of the whales' speech patterns, extraneous thoughts faded, and she tucked frustration away. There was too much going on to allow her focus to be scattered.

She jumped, startled when Don sauntered in carrying a miniature camcorder, the thumb of his free hand in a belt loop at the front of his jeans, a smile on his face, and a question on his lips. "What are you doing in here?" he asked, slouching in the doorway. "I expected to see you out on the point."

"I'm . . . working," she said, then shut up. Her voice was about to give her away. Too many emotions blocked her throat, not the least powerful of which was overwhelming awe at how good he was to look at, even in the middle of the night. She couldn't find her voice, could only gaze at him. His dark gold hair was tousled, his shoes were untied. A rough growth of whiskers glinted reddish on his chin, and he should have looked like a reprobate. He did look like a reprobate, but one whose eyes shone with excitement as he shouldered himself upright in the doorway and strode to where she stood.

"I thought you'd be out there, Trace!" he said.

"How could you miss it? It's the most spectacular sight I've seen in years."

"I've got enough to do in here," she said, waving her hand at the mess she'd already created, the papers spread on her desk, tacked to the wall above it, and even lined up on the floor. Suddenly, foolishly, she wanted to collect all her notes, hide them, deny all knowledge of them.

Her every sense screamed "Intruder alert!" but before she could say anything more, he was right beside her, his eyes glued to the pages on her desk. She searched his face for a sign that he was about to pounce and stab his finger out in accusation: Who *really* wrote that last paper from BIO Research Station?

All he said was "Looks like you could use a decent spectrum analyzer."

"Sure," she said, striving for a casual tone. "There are lots of things we could use. Got any long-range helicopters in your overnight bag? I understand they're great for tracking whales."

He laughed and picked up a stack of papers she'd piled beside the printer, perching on the corner of her desk to leaf through them. "It might surprise you to learn exactly what I have in my overnight bag," he said with a sidelong glance at her.

"It might at that," she agreed, suspecting a hint of innuendo she was determined to ignore.

She stepped around him to pick up a set of headphones so she could monitor the sound waves picked up and transmitted by one of the hydrophones she'd spent weeks anchoring earlier in the year. When the whales she was listening to moved out of range, she took off the headphones and smiled at him.

"But since one of those overnight-bag items *isn't* a real time spectrum analyzer, I'll have to make do with Dad's old-fashioned methods, which means I need my desk back—if you please."

"If you insist." He stood, twirled her chair around, and offered it to her. "While you draw your pretty little pictures of what you conceive as the written language of orcadom, do you need some help keeping this madhouse in order?"

Tracy shook her head. "No, thanks. I'm quite capable of doing my job unassisted. You should go to bed. You have a long way to travel tomorrow, if you mean to get home in one day."

"I wasn't questioning your competence, Tracy," he said evenly.

She compressed her lips, annoyed with herself for having sounded defensive. "I know that. Sorry."

"And as to my traveling," he continued, "did I forget to mention that I'm just beginning the second week of a three-week vacation?"

"Yes, well . . ." If that hadn't been the most blatant fishing for an invitation she'd ever heard, she didn't know what was. She also didn't know what to say. Finally, with a shrug, she answered as noncommittally as she could. "All right, help if you want."

It would be pointless, wouldn't it, to try to keep a man of his background away from what was going on right now? Even if he'd left active research behind several years earlier, she knew he'd kept abreast of the field. He had to, since the Meteor Foundation gave so much of its funding to marine mammal research the world over.

And she did need all the help she could get.

"If you really feel like it, that is," she added, not wanting him to think he was obliged to assist her simply because he was there. She gestured at the camera he'd set on the corner of her desk. "But wouldn't you rather stay outside and catch them in action instead of listening to their sounds in here?"

He cocked one eyebrow. "You mean, play tourist?"

"That's what you are," she said mildly, heading for one of the instruments across the room. "You're on vacation. And since your time here is so limited, you should make the most of it."

"Funny," he said right behind her. "I thought we had that sorted out. I'm in no hurry to go anywhere, and you said you were going to Campbell River only if the whales didn't come. Since they did, and you're not leaving, why not let me stay on a bit longer? Have I outworn my welcome so soon? Do you need my cabin for someone else? I'll happily pay room and board, if that's what it takes. Tracy, don't send me away, not when the whales have just come in. I promise I won't get in your way."

She would dearly have loved to have said yes, his welcome was worn out, or yes, she needed the space he was taking up, but how could she? It wasn't as if there wasn't plenty of room. There was no shortage of food, and he was more than capable of entertaining himself while she was busy with her work. As house guests went, he wouldn't be a problem under ordinary circumstances.

But these were not ordinary circumstances.

Sometime between then and morning, she was going to have to come up with a valid and tactful reason to get rid of the man without arousing his suspicions.

"It would help," she said, "if you'd make a big pot of coffee."

Don headed for the kitchen, thinking of other nights he'd sat in that same workroom sharing coffee with the professor and, sometimes, the young Tracy, until her father chased her off to bed.

He came back, carrying the pot and two cups, plugged it in to keep warm, and took her some.

"Thanks," she said, giving him a quick smile and a glance from under her lashes. "If you'd like to check input on those recorders over there on the east wall, you should hear R pod. They were angling across Queen Charlotte Strait the last time I checked, close to the Numas Islands hydrophones, so they should be near the ones off Twin Islets by now, probably overloading the input limits."

"Right." Don crossed the room to the recorders she'd motioned him toward. The needles bounced erratically, too often going well up into the red zone. He adjusted one, then another, until all three were recording within optimum limits set by Dolby, but knew that it wouldn't last. As different whales passed the hydrophones that fed material to the recorders, further adjustments would be required.

Without being asked, he moved on to the next bank of recorders, noting the marine charts on the wall above and their correlation to what was happening both on the recorders and in the ocean. Numbered spots on the charts corresponded with the numbers on the recorders, telling him where each hydrophone was located. The summer he'd worked with Professor Maxwell, they'd gone rushing out in boats with their hydrophones whenever a pod appeared. Now, it seemed, the pickups were permanent fixtures, anchored at different depths and in many locations on the whales' known routes, transmitting their signals on narrow bands.

"When did you start planting hydrophones?" he asked, and received no reply.

He slid a glance at Tracy. She was intent on her own work, headphones clamped to her ears, and seemed to have forgotten his presence.

She was dressed differently from when he'd left her, so presumably she'd gone to bed and then awakened, as he had, at the first sound of the whales. Her loose cotton pants and wide-necked baggy knit shirt gave her a waiflike appearance, as if she were wearing a larger person's clothing.

Her hair, released from its braid, swirled around her shoulders and hung halfway down her back. As he watched, she shoved it away from her face, pulled it back behind her left headphone, then, as if sensing his stare, she turned and met his gaze for a second. She uncovered her ears. "Sorry. Did you say something?"

He repeated the question. "A couple of years

back," she said. "We set them out in April and bring them back in around the end of August, and hope there aren't too many storms in between. They're pretty delicate, and expensive to replace."

He looked hard at her, trying to read her face, trying to decide if she was angling for information about the status of her father's grant application. It intrigued him that she hadn't mentioned it, not even by hint or innuendo. The omission made him wonder again if she and her father weren't getting along, if perhaps the old man hadn't even told her about the possibility of further funding for their work.

With another faint smile, she glanced away and was gone from him again, bending over the intricate symbols that seemed to capture her entire focus. Did her total concentration come from her love of what she was doing, or did she work so hard in an attempt to overcome the barrier of substandard equipment and lack of assistance?

Substandard equipment and lack of assistance that was soon to become a part of BIO Research's past.

Again he considered telling her his real reason for coming. What would it hurt? And, he reasoned, if anything would shake her out of her refusal to try to contact her father, that would surely do it. Then the professor, drawn by the sums Don had to offer, might decide to return quite soon. That, of course, would mean Don would have to wait for him. It would be worth telling her, if only for that.

He thought about it for a few more minutes. He really should hand the news to the professor before he told anyone else, but hell, Tracy was the old man's assistant. They'd worked together for years. Who had a better right to know than she?

Was he, Don finally asked himself, trying to justify telling her because he thought the news might win him points with Tracy on a personal level? He pushed the idea away with a silent, impatient snort. It wasn't worthy of him. Nor of Tracy.

His next few attempts at conversation met with monosyllabic answers, so he left off, soon becoming so absorbed himself that he all but forgot where he was, unaware of the passage of time. Periodically, one of them would notice that the coffeepot was empty and make more, but their cups usually grew cold and got dumped.

It wasn't until Tracy leaned back in her swivel chair and groaned, rubbing the back of her neck, that he realized it was daylight. From the angle of the sun, he thought it must have been daylight for hours. *He* nearly groaned as Tracy stretched her arms up and arched her back, thrusting her breasts out. She wasn't wearing a bra.

He must have made some sound, because she turned and gave him a startled glance, then froze in position.

For a moment the very air went still, the sounds emanating from the equipment muted, faded away until all Don could hear was the rushing of blood past his ears, all he could feel was the heavy, growing need within him, and all he could see was Tracy, her eyes big and brown and luminous, pleading with him to—to what? To come to her? To stay away?

An aching hunger to touch her, taste her, make love with her, overcame him. He took a step toward her, and she dropped her arms, wrapping them around herself protectively, lowering her head, bringing her hair forward. It shielded her face as she bent over her desk as if to study the paperwork littering its surface.

Everything in Don rebelled at her swift dismissal of what had passed silently but potently between them. She was shutting him out again, hiding behind the exigency of a manufactured chore. The whales were all but still now, most of the pods resting after their long treks, emitting only occasional bursts of sound. Damn, but she intrigued him! Everything about her raised so many questions, he couldn't conceive of them being answered in two lifetimes.

Still bent over her desk, she rubbed the nape of her neck, then one shoulder, and tossed her hair back before concentrating again on her work.

The sight of her long, slender fingers on the skin of her neck made his own hand burn. In a few more long paces he was behind her, inserting his forefingers into the silky dark curtain of her hair, parting it, sliding it forward out of his way.

She jumped at his first touch and flung her head back. A light, sweet perfume arose from her hair as his thumbs stroked over the satin skin of her nape.

"Your neck's all tightened up," he said, gently pressing the muscles beside her spine. "Let me fix it for you."

He felt as much as heard her sigh as he massaged the taut muscles in her shoulders. He deepened the rub, feeling her begin to loosen up. "Lean back," he said, tilting her head against his stomach and massaging down her upper arms, then back toward her shoulders. He stroked a soft touch up the front of her neck to below her ears, circling his fingertips firmly against her jaw hinges, then over her temples.

When she would have moved, he soothed her. "No, let me do this for you. Stay still."

Her breath escaped in a long, tremulous quaver, and her eyelids fluttered open as she looked at him briefly, lashes flickering halfway up before sinking shut again as he stroked down and out to the tips of her shoulders again. "Lord . . . you really know what you're doing, don't you?"

"Feel good?" he asked.

She hummed in assent, letting him continue, but presently she lifted her head, rolling it around and around, and shrugged her shoulders within his clasp.

"Thanks," she said briskly. "I needed that. Sit down and I'll do the same for you."

"Not a chance," he murmured. Touching her was torture enough, though one he wasn't about to pass up. Having her touch him would be too much. "I'm not finished here yet." He began a light pummeling action across the tops of her shoulders.

She didn't argue and he continued.

"Where did you learn to do this?" she murmured, her eyes opening sleepily when he began to massage her scalp.

He smiled. "Trade secret, but someday, if you're a very good girl, I'll give you the full body massage."

"Mmm," she crooned five minutes later when he began working his way down her arms again. "Hey, honey, wanna move in with me?" she asked jokingly.

The unexpectedness of her question jolted a laugh out of him, then he sobered almost as fast at the sudden, strong urge to say yes. Instead, he said, "You're not supposed to ask me that until after I've done the full body massage."

He watched her lips curve in a smile of delight as he drew his fingertips up under her chin and across her cheeks in feather-light strokes. "I don't think I could stand it," she said.

"Sure you could."

She didn't argue the point.

Her facial and shoulder bones felt fine and delicate under his hands, and there was so much more of her he wanted to explore. He doubted he'd ever get enough of touching this woman. *Let me do this for you.* He nearly laughed aloud. If this massage was helping her relax, that was fine, but he was not, most emphatically not, doing it for her—and he was finding it anything but relaxing.

He only wished she would let him go on touching her for the rest of the day. He closed his eyes and began to memorize the feel of her skin beneath his hands.

"Tracy," he said simply because he liked to say her name. But as if his speaking had broken a spell, she jerked herself out from under his hands, spun her chair in a half circle, and jumped to her feet.

"I smell bacon," she said. "Let's go get some before Con eats it all." With an almost panic-stricken glance aimed over her shoulder in his general direction, she bolted toward the kitchen.

Tracy skidded to stop in a kitchen redolent of frying bacon, suddenly aware that she'd been on the verge of running. She hadn't run in the house since she was ten years old. She was acting like a lunatic, and all because of the way Don had said her name. And because of the expression she'd caught on his face when she opened her eyes.

Lord! When had she ever seen such a look of hunger on a man's face? His patent desire unnerved her, because it, too, closely resembled the longing gnawing at her. It had been too easy to let him stride into the workroom and pitch in with help she badly needed, and all too simple to let him stay, work by her side, throughout the hours of the night.

They'd spoken rarely. Mostly, their conversation had consisted of her quiet responses to his occasional questions, and sometimes his answering her queries—all business, colleague to colleague. Yet, it had been one of the most emotionally intense nights she had spent, with her personal awareness of him growing as each hour passed.

That might explain why it had felt so right to lean back into his massaging hands and let him ease the pain in her stiff shoulders. It was crazy, this desire to let him touch her, to ache for it, to put herself into a position where she knew it would happen!

Like before, she wanted him to want her.

If they ever unleashed their passion on each other, where would it end?

She wasn't sure she wanted to know.

"Good morning, Con," she said carefully as the big woman emerged from the pantry carrying two bottles of syrup and a bowl of apples in one arm, and what had to be at least a ten-pound frozen roast in the other.

Con shot her a baleful glare and thumped her load onto the counter before ladling batter onto a hot griddle. "What the hell was all that racket in the night?" she demanded. Con was never at her best before nine in the morning, though to Tracy's surprise, it was already nearly ten. "People banging on my door, yelling at me to get up."

"People?" Tracy echoed. "Dammit, that wasn't *people*. That was me. And I was yelling at you to get up because I needed you!"

"Pah! You didn't need me."

"I most certainly did! I can't believe you simply ignored me, Con. What if I'd been shouting at you to get up because the house was on fire?"

Con shrugged her massive shoulders. "It wasn't."

"No, but six pods came through last night, and I was hopping like a pond full of frogs trying to keep up with everything all by myself." Tracy lifted the slices of bacon from the pan and set them to drain on a platter lined with paper towels.

"All by yourself, huh?" Con snorted. "I knew you'd remember eventually that you had a better assistant than me waiting in the wings."

"Don's a guest. I wasn't about to wake him up at three-thirty in the morning and put him to work," Tracy protested.

"No?" Con grinned wickedly. "That's not the way it looked when I last poked my head in that door half an hour ago. That boy was workin' *hard*, and lovin' it."

Gazing beyond Tracy, she laughed wickedly and said, "Look at that blush, willya?"

Tracy turned instinctively to find that Don's face was indeed flushed. "What's the matter, sonny?" Con went on. "That's an awful guilty look you're wearin'. Guess your thoughts weren't as pure as they shoulda been, huh? Fallin' for a set of fluttering lashes. Pah! I thought better of you."

What Tracy saw was not guilt on Don's face, but a blend of embarrassment and chagrin. She had to laugh. She felt sorry for him. *Almost.*

Con clapped her hands. "Now, let's get going here, people. The day's wasting away."

No one moved. Tracy continued to laugh silently, gazing into Don's eyes, then fluttered her lashes outrageously. His eyes flashed, threatening her, warning her of punishments in store if she didn't behave, but she couldn't stop laughing.

"Set the table," Con barked, and Tracy collided with Don in mid-kitchen as they both leapt to obey.

" 'Used' to be scared of her, huh?" she murmured

as his hands clamped over her shoulders, steadying her.

He grinned, hugged her tightly for the briefest second, then let her go. Suddenly the world was a better place than it had been for a long, long time.

FIVE

Together, Tracy taking things from cupboards and drawers and handing them to Don, they set the table.

Forty-five minutes later, after shaking his head to refuse more of Con's superb coffee, Don followed Tracy out onto the sundeck off the dining area. "What are your plans for the rest of the day?" he asked.

Her plans . . . For one, Tracy needed to phone Edie and see how everything was, but that required a few minutes of privacy.

"First," she said, "I'm going to shower and change, and then I'm going out there—" She waved a hand at a pod of whales foraging halfway between Blackfish and Hansen islands.

"Sounds interesting. May I join you?" he asked with an arched eyebrow and an impudent grin.

"In the first activity, no." She wasn't certain about letting him join her in the boat either.

"Well, darn. Not even if I promised you that full body massage?"

His grin was too infectious. "Not even then," she said.

"You're a hard woman, Tracy Maxwell."

"So they tell me."

He liked the way her eyes danced with laughter. "But you look soft," he said, and stroked a finger over the sun-warmed skin of her satiny cheek, down her jawbone, then brushed her lower lip with the pad of his thumb. "And feel soft." He ran his finger under her chin and along the other side of her jaw, watching her draw a deep breath. Her smile faded. Her eyes darkened from brown to black. Her lashes fluttered down toward her suddenly pink cheeks.

His hand trembled. He snatched it back, shaken by the depths to which she stirred him.

"Okay," he said. "Shower and change for you first. For me, shower, shave, and change. I think we're on the same wavelength."

Tracy thought so too, and scrambled mentally for a way off that one. She was in bigger trouble than she had thought even an hour ago. Each moment in Don's company only added to the wild attraction she had always felt for him. But short of telling him to leave—which she wasn't at all sure he'd do—probably the best move was to let him be with her but keep him physically apart.

A drysuit should do it.

"Is your diving certification still in effect?"

His face split into a wide grin. "Damn right! Are we going *diving* among the whales?"

"I am, and since you're here, I may as well put you to work. Ever made underwater videos?"

"Several times," he said, his eyes sparkling with interest. "Though never of wild orcas."

"Now's your chance. Okay, meet me in the compressor shack in"—she glanced at her watch—"twenty minutes?" He nodded, and she ducked back inside while he jogged down the steps to the path below.

Edie came to the phone at once, and with good news. Their father had settled into the new routine with surprising ease. "He's fine. More than fine, really," Edie said. "He recognized both Wanda and Harry, and is right now shelling peas quite happily on the veranda with Harry. Last night he beat Wanda at a game of chess." Tracy was thrilled to hear it. Wanda was more often unbeatable than otherwise.

"Dad and Harry are planning to go fishing tomorrow. Harry's promised him a tyee," Edie continued, "if it takes all next week for them to get one. If he stays as alert as he is today, there's no way he'll forget about that."

"That's great!" Tracy said, then went on to tell her sister about the superpod forming, and her burning desire to get out there and eavesdrop and maybe even butt in on some of those cetacean conversations, and to get some more footage in the can.

"Tracy, don't you go diving alone!" Edie's voice was sharp, and Tracy understood the reason behind her sister's fear.

"I won't," she said. "You know I won't. I promised you that before you left, Edie. Don't worry. You're not going to lose me too."

"I know you promised," Edie said, "but I also know how tempted you must be. A superpod!"

"There is plenty of data to be collected from the surface," Tracy reminded her sister, but Edie really wasn't interested in that.

"How was your visit with the great golden, gorgeous Don Jacobs?" she asked. "Did you vamp him onto his knees and then laugh while he crawled away?"

"I didn't vamp him. Listen, Edie, I really have to go now. There's so much to do."

"Ah, Trace, I feel so guilty, leaving you with all the work while I'm sitting around eating fresh strawberries out of Wanda's garden. Maybe we should come home today."

"And deprive Dad of his first big salmon in years?" Tracy protested. "No way."

"You shouldn't have to work all alone."

"I, uh, won't be all alone. Not today, anyhow. Don's . . . that is, Con sort of invited him to stay last night, but he spent most of it helping me log the whales in, so I don't have the heart to throw him out today. I know how disappointed he was not to see Dad. The whales arriving when they did is probably all that will make it up to him. I'm supposed to be getting ready to go on a dive with him right now."

"Oh-ho!"

"Now, don't you 'oh-ho' me! It's exactly as I said. I

didn't invite him, Con did. But I must say, I'll appreciate his assistance today as much as I did last night. I'm sure he'll be leaving tomorrow, then you and Dad can come home just as soon as that big fish is on ice."

She hung up soon after that and rushed through her shower, but with a lighter heart than she'd had in ages.

It was too long since their father had showed any sign of enjoying anything. She swallowed hard, wanting to let herself hope that all the doctors they'd taken him to had been wrong, that sometimes miracles did occur.

She knew, though, that there was no hope. Still, while there might not be hope for a recovery, if the rate of decline grew less precipitous, they might have what was left of their father for just a little longer.

Tracy slowed the Zodiac as soon as she spotted whale spouts and maneuvered until they were half a mile ahead of a slow-moving pod. With one eye on the lazily drifting whales, who appeared to be at rest, only the juveniles showing much animation, Don watched her set up her equipment with swift, practiced efficiency.

She slid a glance at him. "In case you're wondering, yes, what we're doing today is trying to prove Professor Maxwell's crackpot 'call them and they'll come' theory. Bet you never thought you'd be in on one of his experiments."

"I've been in on several, if you'll recall," he said,

careful to keep his manner mild in light of her defensive tone. "Including some that attempted to shed light on that very 'crackpot' idea. I realize you don't agree with that assessment of it, though, so if you're willing to spend your time trying to prove your dad's dream can come true, I'm willing to spend mine lending a hand." *Especially if it means spending some more time with you. And the whales, of course.*

"It's more than just a dream," she said curtly, unzipping the bag that held many of the smaller pieces of equipment. He recalled Con's asking Tracy, *What about your dream?* and wanted to ask the same question.

Before he could speak, she clamped on a set of headphones and turned away from him, lowering a hydrophone over the side. Don picked up the other set of headphones and listened intently to the whale song floating eerily through his mind. Was there intelligence behind the whales' vocalizations? Could humans ever interpret the sounds, ever make sense of them and use the animals' own phrases, or any other language, to communicate?

During his lifetime, man had learned to communicate with primates, using electronics and sign language. Captive whales and dolphins—and he knew killer whales were the largest of the dolphins—obeyed commands, interacted with humans, and appeared to enjoy it. And all for the reward of a few hundred pounds of fish a day.

Wild orcas, though, didn't need to have their fish provided, and likely wouldn't thank anyone for offering it. So trying to communicate on any meaningful level with them was, in his opinion, nothing short of a waste of time. Luckily for Professor Maxwell, the majority of the Meteor Foundation's board members had come around to believing that his oft-maligned theory merited further study, hence the awarding of the grant.

But Don knew it was no more than a speculative hypothesis; it might never be more than that, and he hated seeing Tracy wasting her life and talents chasing a dream—especially one that wasn't even her own.

After a few minutes listening, Tracy took off her headphones. As he did the same, she said, "That's A-1. Will you pass me the tape box, please?" She selected a tape she'd prepared in advance, fit it into the player, and tuned the transmitter to broadcast it on a narrow frequency.

"Now comes the fun part," she said, her eyes shining. "Suit up."

Don kicked off his shoes and complied eagerly, tugging the thick neoprene dry suit up over his jeans. This would be his first time diving among whales. Sparing a second for a glance at the huge shapes now only a few hundred feet away, he couldn't suppress a surge of apprehension.

"They won't hurt us," Tracy said, interpreting his glance. "I've been down with them many times. All they express is mild curiosity."

"I'm sure that's true," he said, turning her so he could draw the heavy zipper across her shoulders to seal her suit. "But they're called killer whales for a reason."

"Sure," she said, "the reason being that when they were saddled with that name, nobody understood them. They're no different from many land animals who live by predation, like lions or wolves. They kill to eat.

"All right, yes," she said, holding up a hand to forestall the argument she must have seen rising in him. "They've been seen toying with their prey, sometimes taking hours to kill it. I believe, my dad believes, and a lot of others do too, that they're teaching their young how to hunt."

She turned him around and tugged the zipper that closed his suit across the back of his shoulders. After checking his floatation vest and her own, she handed him a weight belt, then strapped on hers. Though she had checked the tanks and regulators before leaving the wharf, she gave them another once-over.

Don held hers for her as she shrugged into the harness, then slipped on his own.

He hefted the underwater video camera and checked it. "Ready?" Tracy asked, and he nodded. She waved him to the side and he tumbled over backward into the water. Seconds later, before he was stable enough to focus the camera on her, she followed him.

She carried a small underwater transmitter in her hand, hooked to a battery pack she carried in a mesh sample bag fastened to a ring on her suit. Facing him at a ten-foot depth, she signaled to ask if all was okay, and he gave her a thumbs-up. Returning it, she led the way. They moved off together, in a direction they hoped would intercept the whales, Don remaining several yards behind her, filming her as she swam.

Over her shoulder, Tracy saw that Don panned the camera slowly from left to right, up and down, searching, always searching. She did the same with her eyes, constantly on the alert for any kind of motion, knowing how easy it would be to miss an entire pod of whales despite their vast size. Visibility was around thirty feet, and submerged whales moved with an almost unearthly stealth.

Periodically, she thumbed the button that activated the transmitter, letting loose a brief burst of squeals. "Calling them," hoping they'd respond. As she swam, at irregular intervals she transmitted the phrase she had chosen to use that day. This method of trying to reach the whales had been tried before by many researchers, but the phrase she was playing for the whales was one she had carefully chosen, isolated from dozens of recordings made over a period of years. It was one used exclusively by this pod, and one they used frequently; it changed little from year to year.

She needed to learn if they'd respond when it came, not from within their midst, but from farther off, and if they'd come to investigate.

Don marveled at her persistence, at the strength of her belief that her father was right.

As they approached a reef rising sharply below them, he angled the camera down, following the path of a ling cod until it disappeared around a weed-covered outcropping. Small fish darted between fronds of weed, a school of perch, a single rock cod, the latter so well camouflaged by its markings it was visible only because it moved.

He was still trying to track it when Tracy's gloved hand brushed past the front of the lens, and he came to an abrupt halt as a whale appeared suddenly out of the gloom.

Tracy's breath caught as the large black and white shape loomed up not ten yards away. Holding up a hand to stop Don, just barely feathering her fins to maintain her position, she shut off the transmitter, listening for a response, watching intently as the whale ghosted closer. It was joined by another. Though it was difficult to tell, she thought they were both juvenile males.

Carefully, she thumbed the button, broadcasting the phrase again. The whales before her came to a full stop and slowly, so slowly it was almost imperceptible, began to sink, each with an eye fixed closely on her and Don. She adjusted the valves that controlled her buoyancy, saw him do the same, and they sank too, keeping level with the animals. He kept the camera focused on them.

Periodically, she sent out another burst of taped sounds, doubts eating away at her confidence as the whales continued to simply hang there, unresponsive.

Was the sound she transmitted—were most of the whales' phrases—nothing more than identification sounds, as most orca researchers believed, or something more complex, as her father preferred to hypothesize?

The whales were suddenly closer without her having noticed their moving; all at once they were much, much larger, and still very intent on her. She gave them another burst, and they halted as one, staring, she thought, in startled question.

She exchanged a glance with Don, wanted to laugh at his stunned expression, and grinned around her mouthpiece.

Don saw that grin, hoped the camera had picked it up, along with the triumph and jubilation it expressed as it leaked a stream of silver bubbles from around her regulator mouthpiece.

At a depth of fifty feet, the whales stopped sinking, both turning so that their heads were aimed directly at the humans as if they might be about to charge.

A frisson of something approaching fear rippled through Don's body, though he knew no story of an orca attacking a human in the wild had ever been substantiated. As if she suspected his nervous response to the animals' attitude, or shared it, Tracy reached out with her thickly gloved hand and took his. She hung on to his fingers tightly, never for a second taking her eyes off the whales.

What, he wondered, if Tracy's broadcast call had said something like "Soup's on, come and get it," and those two thought he and Tracy were the main ingredients?

But no. He sensed nothing in these beasts beyond mild curiosity. They continued to watch, no doubt wondering what those small swimmers were, and how a call clearly of their own language came to emanate from aliens.

Tracy sent out the call again, and—was it her imagination, a bit of the anthropomorphism she tried hard to squelch each time it arose, or did one of those whales actually lift its head in response?

A sudden burst of sound through the water made her start, though she had heard similar sounds many times before. Never had she heard it at such close range. It rang in her ears, seemed to vibrate through her sinuses and in all her bones, and as it faded, she triggered the transmitter once more. After a pause, the live call was repeated. She was sure it was repeated exactly.

Oh, if only she could know what they were saying! Slowly, still holding Don's hand, never taking her eyes off them, she began to swim back from them, gradually opening the distance. Again she hit the transmitter key. Once more one of the animals responded vocally. She stopped moving, waiting, silently willing them to come to her, to come with her.

They hung back. She played her call again. They remained perfectly still.

This time, the *squee-ee-ee!* she received in response seemed to her to have a distinctly questioning tone to it. Her heart raced as one of the whales moved, seemed about to follow her, and then, as if changing its mind, appeared to levitate, rising upward through the water until it was nothing but a huge black and white blur lost in the streams of her and Don's bubbles.

Distantly, she heard a different call, and realized it came from farther off. The other whale hung suspended above her, staring at her, then it, too, showing no visible means of propulsion, eased away from her to lose itself in the dim green glow of surrounding water.

For several moments Tracy hung suspended, looking longingly through the water, hoping the whales would come back. They had been curious, that she knew. The last one had wanted to stay and figure her and Don out. She knew that. A child being called home by mother couldn't have left new playmates—or a circus freak-show attraction—with more obvious reluctance.

Don't worry, she told it. *I'll be back.*

But, she wondered, would *it*? Had it been, in truth, a child called away from possible danger by a mother determined to protect her young?

Her sigh sent another gush of bubbles aloft, and she became aware that she still clung to Don's hand. They exchanged a long look through their faceplates and then, as she gestured at the surface, began to rise as one.

They followed their bubbles upward, angling back the way they'd come, until they were ten feet below the surface. Tracy halted Don there, one hand on the Zodiac's anchor line as they waited out the decompression time of the nitrogen bubbles in their blood.

When they finally broke through the rippled silver of the water, not a whale was in sight.

Back aboard the boat, they ate their lunch and fed the sea gulls the crusts. Don lay back against the side of the inflatable, stretched his legs out, and gazed up at the blue sky, the puffy white clouds and the wheeling, screaming gulls. "A guy could get used to a life like this," he said. "Real easy and real fast." He closed his eyes, listening to whales breathing at varying distances on all sides.

"Don!" Tracy's whisper and the touch of her bare toes on his ankle brought his head up. "Shhhh," she said, and gestured to something behind him.

Slowly, he sat up and turned, then caught his breath at the sight of a juvenile orca that had poked its head and half its body out of the water, finning with its front flippers, turning in a rapid circle, "spy-hopping," as the activity was known. The sun glinted off its clean white underside, drew attention to the sharp delineation between black body and white eye-patches, and painted a rainbow into the steam of its breath.

Tracy raised her still camera and got off a couple of quick shots. Don brought the camcorder into play while the animal worked its way higher and higher out of the water until it was all but standing on its powerful tail flukes. At that point it flung itself sideways and fell back to the water with a massive splash that sent spray flying in all directions.

They shared a smile and, for a moment, as he lifted a hand to wipe drops of saltwater from her cheeks, Tracy thought Don was going to kiss her. Her lips tingled, her nipples hardened, her throat felt full, but though his eyes darkened, all he did was draw his fingertips down her cheek, then tap her on the chin with a gentle fist.

"What's it going to cost me for some of that underwater footage of yours?" he asked. "That, along with what I have here"—he patted the camcorder, then wiped a few water drops off it—"is going to go a long way toward making up to my son for my not bringing him with me."

"It's not going to cost you a thing," she said. "I think you've earned it." She smiled and popped the top on a soft drink can, handing it to him. "Tell me about Eric."

"He's a great kid," he said, and to his later chagrin, didn't shut up for the next thirty minutes. When he finally did, with apologies, Tracy only laughed.

"A father's entitled to be enthusiastic about his son."

"And you, Tracy? What are you enthusiastic about?"

She stared at him as if he'd grown another nose. "Whales," she said. "What else?"

He smiled and murmured "What else?" as she started the engine and put the boat into motion. As they cruised slowly in search of another pod, Don sat remembering the enthusiasm with which she'd spoken of her future plans when he'd had lunch with her and the professor during that conference in San Diego.

"Someday I'm going to take my show on the road," she'd said, leaning across the table, her face aglow, her eyes alight. "I have literally miles of videotape that I want to put together as a feature-length film that I can take to elementary schools, high schools, colleges, shopping centers, churches, theaters. I want to show it to government bodies, and to the people who never turn on PBS. I want to reach those who've never heard of Jacques Cousteau or Paul Spong or Graeme Ellis.

"I want them to know the excitement of diving among the whales. I want to show them the mystique of the rubbing beach, to watch with me as the whales congregate there. I want them to see the pods come into Johnstone Strait as separate units, then watch them form into superpods, the way groups of . . . of plumbers or psychiatrists or writers take their separate union locals or chapters to a national conference every year."

She paused and laughed with a glance around the room. "The way marine biologists do."

He'd wanted to capture her laughing mouth and kiss her blind, but her father had been there. And he'd had a wife.

"I want people to see that whales have a culture, a lifestyle," Tracy went on, bringing his attention back to her words. "I'd like everyone to know that there are resident pods, like the ones in Johnstone Strait, who live almost exclusively on salmon. That way, when politicians are allocating salmon stocks—so many to the sports fishing industry, so many to commercial fisheries, so many to Native Americans—they know they need to set some aside for the whales.

"I want to go out into the world and show people a different kind of whale from the one that jumps through hoops, or carries a man on its back, around and around and around in a pool. I want them to know that orcas in the wild have tall, proud dorsal fins, not pitiful, flopped-over things like those they see when they go to the zoo."

Her voice lowered, trembled, and her eyes flooded as she added softly, "I want them to stop calling orcas killer whales to justify in their own minds jailing the animals. I want people to feel the same sorrow, the same agony I feel when I see a captive orca, separated from its family, when it hears it calling, calling, calling, and never getting a reply."

As she finished, her voice died away and she ducked her chin down, folded her arms around herself, then gave her head a rueful shake. "Oh, Lord," she said, looking up, appealing to her father. "Dad, why didn't you kick me under the table or something? You know how I get carried away on that subject."

She flicked an abashed glance at Don. "I've heard students refer to that spiel as 'the Gospel according to St. Tracy.' Forgive me, please."

Before Don was able to form an articulate sentence, the professor laughed and patted her shoulder, while smiling at Don, sharing a joke with him. "Never mind, honey," he said indulgently to his daughter. "Everyone's entitled to a dream, and yours is one of the better ones. One day we'll see it come true too. Probably before mine does."

She'd apologized to Don again, and shortly after that they'd separated to go to different seminars.

He hadn't seen her again until the day before.

But nothing had changed. He still remembered the

passion of her speech, passion he knew must carry over into other aspects of her life, passion he had wanted to harness, direct toward him. Her mouth had tempted him that day. It still did, and her lashes still drove him wild. Again he told himself to keep his distance. She made it easy by keeping hers and retiring early that evening, pleading lack of sleep the previous night.

They worked together all day Sunday, and he thought she was as careful to treat him as nothing more than a respected colleague as he was to treat her that way. They spent the daylight hours making another dive, and setting up a remote camera along the shore in Robson Bight, where Tracy hoped to get film of the orcas rubbing their backs and sides on the bottom.

It was an activity exclusive to the Johnstone Strait resident pods.

Almost daily throughout the summer months, the whales returned to the beaches to rub against the smooth pebbles, lining up along the shore in the shallow water. There, each one might spend up to two hours in the mysterious performance before moving out to make room for a different animal. Little was known of this peculiarity, never observed anywhere else or among any other group of orcas. As each one entered the shallows, it exhaled to lose its buoyancy, then, using its tail as a propeller, moved its back and sides against the rolling rocks. Whether to remove parasites or dead skin, or simply because it felt good, scientists hadn't yet ascertained.

It wasn't until Sunday evening that Don brought

up the subject of her desire for a career educating through film.

"What happened to that idea, Tracy?" he asked. "I was deeply impressed by your enthusiasm, you know, all the fire of it, the eagerness. Many of the things you said that day made me start thinking along new lines. Surely by now you have enough film in the can and you could start putting things together." He reminded her of what her father had said about her dream seeing fruition before his.

She shrugged and shook her head, not meeting his gaze as she fiddled with the remote control. "It's gone the way of most dreams, I suppose. I probably wouldn't have changed anybody's mind anyway, and who needs that kind of publicity?"

"You do, for one," he said, but though she cast a startled glance at him, she laughed and began to roll the film back. Her VCR was old and rewound slowly. Like almost everything else at BIO Research, it needed to be replaced.

"No, we don't," she said, pressing Play to watch the whales in action again. "We're getting along just fine as we are."

Don smiled, thinking of the funding the foundation was about to pour into this place, thinking now not of what it would mean to Professor Maxwell, but of what it would mean to Tracy. Would it provide her with the freedom to leave, to follow her own star? Was it strictly lack of money that kept her isolated here every summer, and forced her to spend the rest of the year teaching college students about clams and tube worms?

He leaned back on the sofa, his gaze resting on her profile. "I possibly shouldn't tell you this, but I'm going to anyway." She slid a sidelong glance at him. "You," he went on, "you personally, and BIO Research generally, are going to be getting along a lot better in the future, Tracy. And, like it or not, you're going to be getting your share of publicity."

That certainly got her attention. She shut off the tape and turned to stare at him. "What publicity?"

He grinned, excited now, eager to see her delight in his news, to share in it. "You see, what I came to tell your father is that the Meteor Foundation has awarded this station the grant he applied for many months ago."

He told her its value, and watched her face lose every vestige of color.

And then she laughed.

SIX

"Hey," he said, reaching for her hands, holding them tightly. "You think I'm kidding. I'm not. It's true, Tracy."

"It . . . can't be." She sounded on the verge of tears. He didn't want her to cry, not even with joy. If she cried, he'd have to kiss her tears away, and if he kissed her at all, he'd keep right on kissing her. The temptation would be too great and—

"Yes. Smile, dammit," he said, dragging his mind out of that track. "Didn't I just give you the best news of your lifetime?"

Within his clasp he felt her hands go icy and moist. She shook her head. "No," she whispered.

Her eyes looked enormous, glazed with shock, still registering stunned disbelief. This was not the reaction he had anticipated.

"Tracy, come on! Snap out of it," he said, trying to joke her past this strange response. "This is funding we're talking about here, for Pete's sake, not execution."

She drew a tremulous breath and let it out explosively, snatching her hands out of his, leaping to her feet. "We didn't apply for a grant!" she said. "We don't want one!"

Don rose, frowning. "Your father did, Tracy. Look, I'm sorry if he neglected to tell you. I can see this is a shock to you, but his application has been in our hands since last December. It's been approved in principle. All I had to do was come here, look around, ask a few questions, and award the first check with all the requisite pomp and ceremony. That's what I meant by publicity."

"My *God*!" She flinched back from him, backing toward the doorway, wrapping her arms around herself. She looked at him as if he'd mounted a harpoon gun on Lyon Head and started picking off whales. "No! No grant. No publicity! Take it back!" she cried. "We don't want it!"

"Take it *back*? Dammit, what in the hell is wrong with you? Your father asked for it. It's been awarded. I can't take it back!"

"You have to! My father didn't apply for anything!" she shouted. "He couldn't have! But if he did, it was a mistake, and there has to be a way to take it back! We do not want it, Don. Believe me, we just *don't*! All we want is for you to go away and leave us alone, for everyone to go away and leave us alone! Take your publicity and . . ."

She wheeled and bolted out and down the hall. He heard her bedroom door slam. He was almost there when the lock snicked loudly, barring his way. What the hell? It was the publicity she was freaking over, not the money. This from the woman who had wanted to "take her show on the road"? It made no sense at all.

He pounded with his fist. "Tracy!" he shouted, then realized the futility of it. She'd run from him, locked him out, rejected what he'd thought was going to be happy news. What the hell kind of scientist ever turned down a grant? What kind of research establishment—especially one as shabby and run-down and as obviously in need as this one—would turn its back on funding? Especially after applying for it?

He leaned his forehead on the wall. He'd blown that one for sure. *Tracy* hadn't presented that application. Her father had. And he'd been completely out of line in telling her about it. Maybe he'd been right earlier. She and the old man had had some kind of falling out.

But if that was the case, why was she bothering to conduct his investigations for him?

Oh, hell! What was going on here?

After a moment, he stood erect and walked away. He turned off the lights, let himself out of the house, and lay on his bed in the cabin, watching a sliver of moonlight move from one side of the wall to the other, before he finally slept.

"Fool! Fool! Fool!" Tracy berated herself under her breath as she sat pounding her fists on the side of her bed. "Idiot!"

She buried her face in her hands. What in the world had she done? She had to have been out of her mind! How was she ever going to explain that wild overreaction? She groaned and squeezed her eyes so tightly shut, she saw red and green swirls in the darkness behind her hands. What she should have done was thank him, and explain quietly but firmly that a grant was not required, and that the money would be better placed elsewhere.

Explain? Explain what? Explain it how? She didn't think he was going to be so easily convinced. Moments earlier, his fist had thumped on her door. Once. He had shouted her name. Once. Since then, she'd heard nothing but her own muttered self-recriminations.

She should have found a tactful way to refuse the funding the Meteor Foundation was offering. She couldn't think of one even now, but if she'd simply kept her mouth shut until she'd spoken to Edie, surely her sister would have found a way out of this mess. Edie was like her mom in more ways than one. She knew how to deal with difficult situations.

Oh, Lord! How in hell had Dad ever written a grant? It was almost impossible to believe he could have done it in one of his few lucid periods since last summer.

December? Don had said the foundation had been in possession of it since last December. She couldn't recall a time in December Dad had so much as recognized her, let alone recognized the need for funding.

What if it were one Mom had written long ago and then forgotten when she fell ill? She supposed it was possible Dad had found it and somehow gotten it out in the mail. Right. That had to be the explanation. It was the only one she could come up with. So fine. She'd explain it that way to Don, and he'd see that it was impossible to—

And there she was again. Explain what? What would he or the Meteor Foundation care who had actually written the grant or when? They'd awarded it on the basis of the way it was written. They'd seen some validity in it.

She groaned again and stripped off her clothes, shivering, though the night was not cool. She put on a flannel nightgown and crawled into bed, but despite that, she continued to shake with cold that came from the inside out.

Maybe she wouldn't have to explain. She'd get up early and sneak away. Maybe she'd ticked him off so badly, he'd be gone by the time her day's work was done.

Her throat closed off. *Without saying good-bye?*

Of course he'd leave without saying good-bye. That's what he'd done last time, when she'd acted like a trollop. And this time she'd acted like a termagant, screamed at him like a fishwife, behaved like a total ass. And why? Through plain, lily-livered panic. Fear.

Publicity. It was that word that had done it.

All she'd been able to see was a mental image of

her father, before a battery of cameras, accepting the check from Don.

And drooling.

More than anything, it upset her when he did that. How he'd hate that loss of dignity, if he was aware of it. Tears burned in her eyes. He'd been drooling the morning the secretary from the Meteor Foundation had called and alerted her to Don's imminent arrival.

The scene rose up before her now.

She'd just finished promising Edie she'd get rid of Donald Jacobs in record time. . . .

"I'll take care of everything at this end. You just take care of—"

"Agnes . . . Agnes, where are you?"

Both women turned at the sound of the querulous voice. "Right here, dear," Edie said, going to her father as he appeared in the hallway, his white hair sticking up all over his head. He staggered slightly.

Tracy watched her sister slide an arm around her father's waist to support him. When he mistook his younger daughter for his wife, neither Tracy nor Edie corrected him. It only confused him and made him angry.

A trickle of saliva slid over the stubble on his chin. Tracy wiped it away with a tissue from her pocket. He flinched back, a suspicious look on his sunken, white-bristled face. "Who are you? What are you doing in my house?"

Tracy clenched her teeth against the pain of his nonrecognition, though she knew it might last only a moment or two—or a week or two. Her heart broke a little more each day, watching him fail.

He had the same strong shoulders, the same powerful build—but he looked somehow . . . diminished. He had the same face as always—but his eyes were vacant.

Robertson Ennis Maxwell, one-time professor emeritus of oceanic studies at Islands West University, renowned for his studies of cetacean species, but most specifically orcas, had his boxer shorts on over his pajama bottoms. One leg was hobbled by the armhole of a life jacket that dragged behind his foot on the floor.

Recalling that scene, Tracy told herself she'd been justified in refusing Don's surprising offer of funding. What she had not been justified in was her method of going about it.

Still, she reckoned she'd kept her promise to Edie. She'd gotten rid of the man.

Promises. Loyalties. Duties.

They sure could screw up a life.

It was not yet six o'clock when Don awoke. No one else would be up, but he rose, his mind already active, churning over with questions, all of which had to do with Tracy.

He made coffee with the supplies Con had put in for him, and as he poured his first cup, he glanced out the window. Tracy, walking purposefully, carrying a thermos and something he couldn't make out, strode up the hill toward the top of Lyon Head.

Where was she going? Obviously, not out in the boat as he'd anticipated. He'd thought she would probably try to escape him that morning, run away and hide somewhere he couldn't follow, the way she'd gone to her room and locked the door. He'd envisioned her spending the day in Robson Bight where, as a scientist at a recognized research station, she was authorized to go, and he was not—at least not in a boat with the markings of a local rental place.

He finished his first cup of coffee. Did her remaining on Blackfish Island, within his reach, mean she'd be willing to talk to him? Willing to explain her incredible reaction to his news? It was time to find out. He refilled his mug, shoved his feet into his sneakers, and followed her.

It was a perfect morning. Tracy walked quickly, squinting into the sun—a perfect morning she was in no mood to enjoy.

Early as it was, she had talked to Edie ten minutes before. Luckily, Edie and Wanda were both up, so she hadn't disturbed anyone. Dad and Harry were off already on the promised fishing expedition. She'd called to tell Edie about Dad's applying for the grant, but after hearing her sister's blithe voice, had held back. Edie sounded happier and more relaxed than she had in a long time. It would be cruel to upset her now. She seemed totally unconcerned over the length of Don's stay, saying, "You handle it any way you think is best. We're just fine here."

She planned to spend the day helping sew a quilt for Wanda's new granddaughter. Tracy suspected her sister would benefit from a few more days under Wanda's TLC.

Edie, she thought as she reached the top of Lyon Head and sat in her favorite position with a view of forever, deserved a break. She sat and poured herself a cup of coffee from her thermos, sipped for a few minutes, then lifted her flute and began to play softly. Sometimes that helped her think, and she had a lot of thinking to do. A lot.

After half an hour and another cup of coffee, she set her flute down and steeled herself for action. Don, like her, was an early riser, or had been fifteen years before. He'd probably be awake now. It was time to go home and face a different kind of music.

Trouble was, she still didn't know what she was going to tell him.

As she continued to procrastinate, she thought with a brief stab of longing of the money his foundation offered, and the new equipment it could provide.

A real-time spectrum analyzer! The ancient analyzer she'd been using for years was a total dinosaur that spent far too much time in the shop. With a new one, all she'd need to do would be feed audiotapes into it and watch images come up on the screen of a color monitor, representative of the tonal spectrums involved. There, she could freeze them, compare them, print them, study them properly.

Oh, yes, she'd almost kill for one of those.

But would she kill her father's hard-earned reputation as a researcher and teacher?

No. No, she would not. She put the flute to her lips and blew across it again. It seemed she still had some thinking to do.

Don heard her music before he actually saw her. She sat in a small declivity, partway down the slope, just at the brink of where it tilted away sharply to fall to the ocean a hundred feet below. He stood above and behind her, listening to her play, watching the breeze tug her curls into wild disarray, watching the sun glint off their ends, turning them to dark flame.

She played, appropriately, "Morning Has Broken," then segued into "Amazing Grace." As the last notes faded away and she set her flute down, Don moved forward.

"Good morning," he said, sitting beside her.

She looked up, startled, her gaze wary. "Good morning."

He slid a hand around the back of her neck, under the thick fall of her hair. "I think we can both do better than that," he said.

He saw confusion cross her face, the question form on her pink lips before she voiced it. "What?"

He covered her mouth in a soft kiss that he wanted to go on and on, but only seconds after her lips trembled apart under his, he pulled back.

"Now, that," he said, "is the right way to say good morning on such a beautiful day." Her smile didn't quite make it all the way to her eyes.

"I've heard that some researchers play the flute

and other instruments for the whales in captivity and they seem to like it. Ever play for them in the wild?"

She nodded. "Sometimes. Dr. Paul Spong, who runs ORCALAB, just over that way"—she gestured at a distant island—"was the first to do it. He even brought in a rock band and floated them down Johnstone Strait to see if the whales would respond."

Don cocked his head to one side. "Did they?"

She shrugged. "I don't think anyone's sure. Sometimes, though, when I'm out in the kayak and they come close, I've played for them and I think they like it. They seem to stay around longer when I do. Or maybe that's just wishful thinking."

He nodded. "Maybe. Play for me. I can guarantee it'll make me stick around. Of course, I will even without that, but I'd like to hear you play some more."

She looked down at her flute. "I owe you an explanation," she said.

He shook his head. "You don't owe me anything, Tracy. My official business here is with your father. I should have waited to speak to him. I will wait until I can, to pursue that issue any further. But the issue of you and—"

She broke in. "Stop. Please. I have to tell you this."

He studied her face, seeing apprehension in her eyes, taut reluctance in the straight line of her mouth, but determination in the set of her chin. "All right," he nodded. "Go ahead."

"My father," she said, "is not in Alaska. He's in Campbell River."

Don tried to smooth out the swift frown that tugged his brows together. "But—"

She didn't let him go on. "He has Alzheimer's," she said in a voice so devoid of expression, she might have been reading an eye chart. "If he applied for that grant, he didn't know what he was doing. He doesn't often know much of anything. Or anyone. Not even me."

Don felt the shock of her words slam into him. "*Tracy* . . ." He tried to lift a hand, to touch her, to offer some kind of comfort, but what good would it do?

She shook her head, and he could see that she'd reject any expression of sympathy from him. It hurt. It hurt more than he'd thought such a thing would. Or could. That there was nothing in the world he could say or do to make the pain stop for her. He saw it in her eyes, in the tense angle of her shoulders, the rigidity of her back as she sat beside him, her flute clutched in one white-knuckled hand.

"His mind started slipping even before Mom got sick," she continued in the same flat tone. "She covered for him as long as she could, making excuses, even to Edie and me, taking on more and more of the tasks he was responsible for, keeping him out of the public eye as much as she could. Only after she absolutely had to, she told us, and once we knew, we started covering for him too.

"It was easy to start with. He'd always had a reputation as the proverbial absentminded professor, so his students and colleagues were willing to accept his forgetting their names, forgetting appointments, forgetting where he was supposed to be at any given moment. Since I was on the same faculty, I was able to stay near him and steer him if he appeared lost. At least," she added, and for the first time her voice trembled slightly, "as long as he recognized me. But about then, Mom died, and he retired."

She rubbed her left knee rhythmically with the tips of her fingers, staring down. Don wanted to stop the compulsive rubbing, wanted to stop the story. He had the picture; he knew enough, and he could see how painful this was for her. The suffering in her voice as she continued brought an ache such as he'd never known to Don's heart. She'd always been close to her father. His forgetting her must have felt like the worst kind of betrayal.

"When it got too risky to keep him where people might realize what was going on, Edie brought him up here to live full-time. Her marriage broke up just after Mom's death, so she needed to get away too. And here we could keep him hidden. That's why I've worked alone these past few years, brought in no one who might . . . talk out of turn."

She fell silent, and for the life of him, Don didn't know what to say.

"So there you have it," she said finally, looking up again, and he saw her eyes were bright with tears she wouldn't shed. "That's the way it's been these past few years. When I learned you were coming here, I sent Dad away to stay with friends. Edie went to look after him. So, as you can see, a Meteor Foundation grant for BIO Research would be totally inappropriate."

She laughed lightly and smiled. "BIO Research has . . . lost its head."

He closed his eyes for a second against the pain her laughter couldn't begin to hide, then wound his arms around her.

"Baby, baby . . ." he murmured against her hair. "I'm so sorry. And you're wrong. Funding is even more appropriate now than ever before. There's no reason you should have to work alone, struggling against all those obstacles. With the grant, most of the immediate pressures will be lifted. You'll have all the assistance you—"

"Don!" Tracy tore herself out of his embrace and shot to her feet, backing away from him, up the slope of the rock. Oh, God, it had felt so good for those few seconds she had let him hold her! It had felt so right. And she felt so bereft without it, but . . .

"Haven't you been listening?" she cried. "Apart from having strangers around upsetting Dad, I can't bring in students, can't let other scientists come here, because the word would get out about his condition. If the scientific community ever learns that his brain died before his body, everyone will put his findings down as the ravings of an ailing man out of touch with reality. That might even call into question other papers of his which have been widely accepted and considered entirely viable bases for further research.

"I don't want to see all his years of work come to nothing, to have to watch it die along with him because no one will believe it could possibly be valid. You know he's had his detractors."

She flung out her hands. "You were one of them, remember? You were the first to publicly dub his theory Professor Maxwell's crackpot *call them and they'll come* notion."

She saw dark color ebb and flow in his face. "Yes," he admitted, standing also. "But I long ago began to rethink that position. Largely through having listened to you in San Diego. Not just those things you said to me privately at lunch, but what you said in the seminar you and your dad gave. I started thinking that maybe he—the two of you—were on the right track. And whether you ever saw it or not, I did publish a paper to that effect a year or two ago."

She hadn't seen it, but that felt good too, hearing him concede such a thing, knowing he had done it publicly. She hadn't known he'd attended their seminar either. It surprised her to realize he had been in the lecture hall and she hadn't sensed his presence.

"A lot of other researchers who once disagreed with your dad now feel the same, Tracy," he continued. "That's why the grant was authorized—because of a growing weight being given his work, a stronger consensus that it should be continued. Supported."

How she wanted to believe that, to believe that her father's illness wouldn't matter, but she couldn't. She knew better. "I'd say some have begun to agree with Dad," she said. "Some, not a lot."

She picked up a broken clam shell dropped by a crow and flung it down the cliff, needing physical activity. "There are still too many who consider it a crackpot idea," she said. "The hobbyhorse of a man so opposed to whales in captivity, he'll say anything, do anything, to convince his colleagues it's not only wrong but unnecessary. But we are going to prove it.

"It's just a matter of time now," she said, stepping closer to him. "Spending time with the whales, transmitting their phrases back to them until I find the right one, the one that will really get their notice, the one that says, 'Listen up, you guys, I'm here and I'm talking to you.' " She looked into his eyes, appealing to him.

"Don't tell anyone about Dad, Don. Please! Find some way to make the foundation take back the grant. Give me the time I need. I'm close! I'm so damned close, I can taste it! Please don't take that away from me, away from him!"

She wrapped her hand around his wrist. "To accept that grant, and the assistants I'd be obliged to hire as a result of it, would be to negate everything I've worked for these past three years, to destroy the very thing that I most want: for Dad to go down in history as the man who first proved it was possible to communicate with whales in the wild, the man who made others think along lines of study beyond what was being done on orcas in aquarium tanks.

"I don't want him to be footnoted in textbooks as nothing more than a once-respected researcher who went to his demented death still ranting about letting captive whales go because they could teach wild whales how to 'talk' to us."

Don gaped and clasped her upper arms. "Oh, hell!" he exploded. "Are you telling me your dad has managed to convince *you* that's possible? It's a completely nutty idea, one I can understand coming from him, given the circumstances, but not you! You must know it's been disproved in dolphin studies, except for the odd anecdotal bit of circumstantial evidence that most serious scientists discount." He shook her lightly. "You're not aiming any of your studies in that direction, are you?"

"And if I said I was?" she demanded, a clear challenge, with hope as its basis. "Would that negate the grant?"

"No," he said. "The grant was awarded to your father. I don't think anything you say can stop it now. Besides, he published a retraction of that idea, saying he'd put it forward only to stir up controversy, and therefore debate, on the issue of whales in captivity."

Tracy shook her head. "I published that retraction under his name."

"I see." He frowned. "Covering up."

She nodded. "Covering up. But doesn't it tell you anything, your own initial reaction to thinking I might believe it? You know it's a crazy idea, just as I do. Knowing it was Dad's crazy idea, and knowing what his mental state must have been when he came up with it, don't you find yourself doubting, just a little, some of his other theories? Wondering how long ago his mind started to deteriorate?"

He said nothing, but continued to frown.

"Can't you see," Tracy went on, "that other people, those who don't know him, who never knew him, might use it to discredit his other theories?"

He sighed gustily and nodded. "Yeah. Okay, I can see what you're getting at."

Tracy slipped away from him. "If I can prove his position before he dies, and continue to keep his Alzheimer's from ever becoming public knowledge afterward, his work will continue to be seen as valid. It will lead to other work on the same lines."

"Such as the work you've been doing on his behalf these past several years."

"Exactly, but not only mine; that of other scientists in other places as well. I have no intention of trying to keep my findings a secret. I want to share them, want other researchers actively involved in investigating the same things with different groups of orcas all over the world. I just don't want them doing it here, with me. Not now."

"Other researchers who will then receive the credit for their findings," he said.

"Of course."

"So let me ask, what about your receiving the credit you deserve for your years of work and study? What if, through your labors, the analysis you're doing on vocalization, you achieve that breakthrough you seek in your father's name? What of your name, Tracy? What of your reputation? What of your position in history books?"

"That doesn't matter," she said, backing away from him. "He's my father. I care about him, and this is what I've chosen to do."

"It matters to me," he said. "As a member of that very scientific community you're trying to hoodwink, it matters, because I see a wrong being done, a lie being told and perpetuated. I see the work being done by one person, see a paper being written by that same person, and see it being published under someone else's name."

Tracy's head went up. "And that offends your oft-noted high moral standards?"

"Yes, it offends me, but—"

"Don't be so damned holier-than-thou, Don!" she cut in, tossing her hair off her forehead. "I'm doing what I *want* to do, and for my own father, not for some stranger who demands it of me as his right of office. If you're so offended, I suggest you go and get offended at the head of every research department in every university the world over, because assistants do the work and department heads take the credit every day. It's been that way for generations in the past, and will continue for countless more in the future."

With that, she snatched up her flute and stalked away. He picked up her thermos and his own cup, and let her go without further argument because he knew she was, at least on that score, absolutely right.

"Tracy." Don's voice startled her when he entered her office later that day. After their early morning conversation on Lyon Head, she had sped away in the Zodiac, spending several hours on the water. She'd more than half expected him to come looking for her in his rental boat, but he'd left her to herself. She'd spent a lot of time trying to pretend she was glad.

At the sound of his voice she swiveled her chair around and faced him, her breath catching as he approached. His long, lean legs had been made for the faded jeans he wore, as tight as the blue T-shirt that showcased his chest and shoulders. He was in his customary pose, with one thumb hooked through a belt loop. His hair looked as if the wind had been at it—or a woman's fingers. Hers itched to smooth it. He smiled, and his eyes crinkled.

"What," he said, crouching before her chair, trapping her in it with his hands on its arms, "what if there were a way for BIO Research to have that grant and no publicity?"

She stared at him and drew a deep breath that smelled of his scent. It made her want to close her eyes, made her want to sway into him. She held herself rigid.

"There is no way," she said. "The standard conditions of that kind of funding require the funded establishment to hire junior researchers and to teach them. Or at least provide an opportunity for them to further their studies."

"There might be a way around that," he said. "I've spent most of the day toying with different ideas, and I think there is a way. If I go back to the board, tell them the truth, explain things as you explained them to me, I'm sure they'll understand the need to keep your father's medical history private. They are all reasonable men and women. I don't see any reason why the standard conditions couldn't be waived under the circumstances."

Hope warred in her with disbelief. "Waived? How? Why would they?"

"Because they trust me," he said, standing and pacing away. "Because they respect my judgment. If I say that we need to put it out that the introduction of new researchers here at this time would jeopardize the bonding between you and the orcas in the pods you're studying, that would be grounds to waive the conditions."

Tracy gazed at him. "Don . . . it might not be true. You know that. You were with me when those juveniles came to see what we were doing. They had never seen you before. They weren't frightened off, and your presence had no apparent effect on their behavior."

He pulled her out of her chair, his hands warm on her shoulders. "We don't know that. And what I say *could* be true," he insisted. "It's a feasible theory. Also, I was only one other diver among them. Would it be detrimental to your studies if there were three more, or six? If there were more boats in the water, complete with their prop noise?"

Tracy stared at him. It hadn't been fully established if boats among them bothered the whales, though current thinking suggested it was better to err on the side of caution and keep human-whale contact to a minimum. What Don said made some kind of sense.

"You think they would agree?" she asked.

He nodded. "I can't promise it, but yes, I think it's possible."

She broke free of his hands and tore at the bonds of surging hope that told her to take a risk, that begged her to believe that risk was minimal.

"No," she said tautly. "No. I can't accept. I don't want the funding. Why can't you go back and say that your on-site inspection forces you to recommend against awarding the grant?"

"It wouldn't be true, Tracy."

"Wouldn't it?" she demanded. "You came here to see if everything was as my father's grant application stated it. It's not, Don! You know that. Everything's different, everything's changed. BIO Research isn't a worthy recipient because Professor Maxwell won't be able to use the funds as the foundation intends."

"But you will," Don said, reading the indecision in her eyes, her longing to take what the foundation offered, doubt that it could work the way he said it would, fear of what it might mean if it didn't. As he watched, he saw that fear win out as clearly as if it had been written in plain English in black type on white paper.

"No!" she said, wheeling away from him. "No. Even if you asked for secrecy regarding Dad's illness, things like that have a way of leaking out. I can't do it, Don. I can't risk it all. I've invested too many years in it now to see it destroyed. I can keep things together without a grant. I have to."

"Tracy . . ." A dozen different arguments raged through his mind, but not one seemed adequate to convince her. She faced him from half the room away, an obdurate expression on her face, waiting for his agreement, maybe even unconsciously pleading with him. "Oh, Trace—"

The relief on her face when the phone rang should have been laughable. It wasn't. It hurt him as much as her refusal to accept his comfort had that morning. It was as if he were another obstacle in her life, another complication to be surmounted in her struggle to complete her tasks in the limited time she had left.

She snatched up the phone, spoke, then handed it to him. "It's for you."

"Oops! The office. You know, I never did call them back." He picked up the phone and said, "Hi, Freddi, sorry, but by the time I remembered I was supposed to call, we were into the weekend and—*Muriel?* What's wrong?"

SEVEN

As a thready, high-pitched voice emanated from the phone, its words unintelligible to Tracy, Don's face creased into a frown, then his mouth opened into an expression of blank disbelief.

"What do you mean, where is he?" he barked. "He's not with me, thanks to you! I—*has* to be? How can you say he has to be? He's not!"

His eyes, wide and shocked, met Tracy's. He rammed a hand agitatedly through his hair. "Dammit, Muriel, he's fourteen years old! *You're* supposed to know where he is! You're his mother and—"

He broke off abruptly in response to a wail Tracy heard easily, making a visible effort to bring himself under control. "All right," he continued, moderating his tone as he stood leaning with one hand on her desk as if needing support. Tracy rolled her chair up against the back of his knees, but though he didn't sit, he captured her hand on its back and held on, seeking human contact.

"I'm sorry," he said tautly into the phone. "That wasn't fair, but he's my son too, and I'm as scared as you are. I'm coming back. I'll charter a plane and be—"

Muriel must have interjected something, because Don listened for a minute, then exploded. "No damn way! How can you expect me to stay *here* when my son's missing somewhere in California? I have to be there to help look for him!"

He let go of Tracy's hand to slam the flat of his palm on the desk. "I don't *know* where! I have to start somewhere, though, and at the beginning of his trail seems logical. What if he didn't follow me? What if he's been kidnapped? I—"

Again his ex must have interrupted. He dropped his head and moaned. "Yeah. Yeah, all right, I see their point, but dammit, they're just cops. I'm his father!" He pounded the heel of his hand against his forehead. "How can you or anyone else expect me to simply sit and wait for him to call?"

He splayed his hand flat on the desk, swaying as if he were about to fall.

Tracy covered his hand with hers; he turned his palm over and gripped her fingers so tightly they ached, but she didn't pull away. He kept his gaze fixed on her face while he listened to his ex-wife, asked several more questions, then hung up.

For several moments he stood there, his face blank, his eyes still registering shock.

He sat abruptly. "My son . . ." She saw his throat work as he looked up at her. "He's run away. They think he's run away. Muriel thought I'd gone against her and brought him with me. I didn't, of course, and now she thinks he's following me. That's the police theory anyway."

"Following you? From San Diego?"

"Yes. Oh, hell!" He thrust himself out of the chair and across the room. He clamped his hands on the windowsill and hung on for a moment, only to push himself violently away and stride back, as if the confinement were too much to bear. "Dammit, this is all my fault."

He drove one fist into the opposite palm. "Why didn't I keep my mouth shut? Why didn't I clear it with Muriel before I mentioned it to Eric? I know what she's like. If she thinks there's something I really want, something she feels might earn me points with Eric, she'll block it even if it means hurting him. And now, because of that, he's in danger of being hurt a hell of a lot worse, hitchhiking nearly two thousand miles all alone."

He groaned and turned to pace the length of the room again.

Tracy thought about the horrors that could befall a hitchhiking fourteen-year-old. Then it struck her. "Don, he can't be following you! He must know he'd never get across the border. If he didn't think of that, and did actually try to come after you, they'll be searching every vehicle crossing between Washington State and B.C. by now. They'll find him."

His tortured expression didn't change. "That's what the police said, but Muriel didn't know he was missing until he failed to show up after supposedly spending a few days camping with friends. He never went with them, which means he left home even before I did. He's had a three-day lead. He could have been across the border before anyone even suspected what he had in mind."

"From southern California to the B.C. border? That's a long way," Tracy said, keeping her tone level, striving to make him see reason and logic. "And once he got to the international boundary, an unaccompanied boy wouldn't be allowed to enter the country."

"What if he doesn't try to come across unaccompanied but hitches in a vehicle with a parent-aged driver? If the person who gives him a ride hasn't asked the right questions, or is unscrupulous or uncaring enough to accept whatever story Eric might have offered, and if the immigration people aren't on the ball, he'll sail right through."

Tracy nodded. Those were a lot of "ifs," but she knew he was right. If Eric were a younger child, maybe the authorities would ask questions. But he was fourteen.

"Your w—his mother is convinced he's headed here? That he hasn't just run away and might be hiding out somewhere to scare her, scare both of you?"

He nodded, his face grim. "I'm convinced, too, that he's coming here, because he wanted it so badly."

"Would he have any idea how to get here?"

He frowned and rubbed a thumb between his

brows as if his head ached. It probably did. "He knows. We started planning a long time ago to buy a boat and cruise up the Inside Passage all the way to Alaska some summer. We've pored over cruising guides and marine charts together. I promised him that we'd stop in here so I could show him around. Hell, I raised him on stories of that summer I spent here. He's begged me to go buy that boat, to make the trip reality, not just a dream.

"So naturally, when I decided to visit this year, I asked him to come with me. He was so eager, so excited, it made the prospect even more inviting for me." A groan escaped him. "And then Muriel said no."

He closed his eyes for a second. "I think he'll find the place all right, so long as nothing happens to him before he can get here."

He blew out a long breath that did little to calm the grinding fear in his chest.

"Don't think about that," Tracy said, wrapping her fingers around his wrist. "Assuming he got rides frequently, how long do you suppose it would have taken him to reach the border?"

He frowned. "I don't know. Three, maybe four days, unless he traveled all night."

"Okay, let's assume he did that, and assume he actually made it across the line before the police were notified. All he'd need to do was take the ferry from Tsawwassen to Victoria and start hitchhiking up Vancouver Island. He could make that trip in less than a day with any kind of luck, so he could arrive in Sointula at any minute. He could already be there, trying to figure out a way to get out here to our island."

Seeing he wasn't convinced, Tracy slid her hand up his arm to the edge of his sleeve, then back down again, her palm making a slight rasping sound over the crisp hairs on his skin. "I know how impossible it'll be for you to sit here waiting for the phone to ring. Come on, there is one thing we can do. Do you have a picture of Eric with you?"

"Of course," he said. He pulled out his wallet and flipped it open, holding it out to her.

She took it in her hands. It was warm from his body, shaped in a curve where it had molded to his hip, and it smelled of leather—and his skin.

The boy smiling up at her from behind the plastic window greatly resembled Don, though his hair was as dark as her own, and his direct gaze revealed large, limpid brown eyes. He had a good, strong chin, like Don's, and a mouth that would, in time, be considered sensuous by a lot of women. His nose just missed the hawklike form of his father's, but would probably achieve it with age.

"He's like you," she said.

He shrugged. "More like his mother's side of the family in coloring, though if shoe size is anything to go by, I think he's going to be as tall as I am." He smiled.

"And a helluva lot smarter," he added. "He's a year ahead in school because he skipped third grade." Pride rang in his tone. "They wanted to skip him past the sixth as well, but I nixed that. He may be as academically advanced as kids two years older than he is, but he's two years younger both emotionally and socially. Maybe more than that."

He closed his eyes for a second, squeezing them tight as if in pain. "He's so damned *trusting*, Tracy! Oh, God! If any son of a bitch hurts him, I'll—"

She reached over and took his hand, his suffering cutting into her. "God, Tracy, he may be fourteen, but he still has a basic childish belief that people are good and kind and want to look out for kids."

"They do," she said. "Most people do and that's what we're going to cash in on."

"What . . . ?"

"Come on," she said, taking his hand and tugging him across the room. "Let's go. We've got things to do."

Don wasn't quite sure why, but he followed her. Maybe it was because whatever she had in mind beat the hell out of sitting around staring at the phone and feeling helpless.

In Port McNeill, on the Vancouver Island side of Johnstone Strait, following a short boat trip and a ferry ride, Tracy introduced Don to her friend Jayne, owner of an office supply and services store. She explained briefly that Don was an old friend and colleague, and about Eric's attempt to follow Don.

"So you see, we need to have this photo enlarged, photocopied, and sent any place any of us can think of that would be a help, like TV stations, ferry terminals, bus depots, wherever. Of course, the police will be doing it too, but they have to go through channels and procedures we don't need to worry about. The more publicity we get, the more often Eric's picture is seen, the sooner someone will spot him and let us know where he is."

"Got it," Jayne said, and went into action.

Later Don stood gazing down at the enlargement of his son's picture, seeing the open innocence in Eric's eyes, the wide grin that never quite faded, the clear enthusiasm for life. He suppressed a groan and concentrated on trying to find adequate words of thanks for Tracy's friend, who had willingly worked long after quitting time to do all she thought was necessary to help get Eric safely home.

She'd insisted that merely an enlargement of Eric's picture wasn't enough, then sat down at her computer and created a banner headline containing all the pertinent information. With the photograph mounted below the information, they had an impressive poster to copy and send to all the applicable places.

If Jayne had had her way, they'd have put an Eric poster on every second telephone pole between there and San Diego. When the job was done, she'd refused to take a cent for any of it, saying, "Hey, I have kids myself. Just promise to let me know when Eric's safe."

"I'll do better than that," he'd said. "I'll bring him in to meet you and if you want, you can give him a thump for all the trouble he's put you to."

"I'll leave that to you. Me, I'll give him a big hug."

Don had to make a concerted effort to keep his

eyes dry. "Me too," he said, praying that it would be so. "Me too."

As if she knew how precarious his emotions were, Tracy hugged Jayne on his behalf, then took his hand and walked in silence to a restaurant near the ferry dock. They had to wait for the next sailing, but in the meantime they could eat, she insisted. Even if he didn't feel like it, he had to try. Otherwise, she'd tell Con.

The threat brought a smile to his lips, and he was surprised to discover that he could eat after all.

With a container of hot chocolate in his hand, Don stood with Tracy at the ferry's railing on the return trip. Facing the brisk wind blowing down Broughton Strait, he stared into the orange and peach clouds that continued to illuminate the long twilight. In those latitudes, and at that time of year, he knew full dark wouldn't come until well after ten o'clock.

Darkness . . .

He remembered how, after the divorce, the then-nine-year-old Eric had developed a fear of the dark. Was he afraid now, with night approaching? How many nights had he spent on the road since he ran away? Three? Four?

Don was filled with terror for his son, and didn't hesitate to admit it to himself. He glanced down at Tracy and caught her comforting smile. She knew. She slipped an arm around his waist and placed a hand on his chest.

She had been as silent as he during dinner, each immersed in their own thoughts. Now she spoke.

"He's going to make it, you know," she said. "I'm sure of it because he's your son. He's smart and resourceful and very likely pretty tough. All you have to do is trust him to look after himself the way you've taught him, while we wait for him to either call or show up. He's going to do one or the other, and he's going to do it soon. I believe that, and I want you to believe it too."

He brought one hand up and covered hers. "I want to," he said. "I'm trying to."

She smiled and slid her hand to the back of his head, pulling his face down and giving him a soft kiss on the corner of his mouth. "Try harder."

He put his free hand in the small of her back and brought her closer, still feeling the light pressure of her kiss. He couldn't remember the last time anyone had kissed him like that—a kiss to make a hurt better. Nurturing, caring.

He realized it was something he had missed.

Tracy stepped away from him, crushed her container, and dropped it into a receptacle. Without the warmth of Don's body close to her, she felt the chill and wrapped her arms around herself to dispel the shivers brought on by the cool breeze. The light jacket she wore over her T-shirt had been fine on the trip over, but now, at the end of the day, it proved inadequate.

"Want to go inside?" Don asked, but she shook her head. Inside would be people she knew, people she'd have to introduce Don to, and she realized he preferred to be alone just then. He put an arm around her again and pulled her close, tucking her back against his front.

She tried to remain friendly but physically unresponsive to his embrace, but he rubbed her arms with his hands, and murmured, "Relax and lean on me. I'm only trying to keep you warm." She complied with another little shiver, this one having nothing to do with the cool wind.

"You make a good windbreak," she said.

"You make good company," he said, his lips close to her ear. "You seem to know instinctively when I want to talk and when I don't."

Her instinct told her that this was one of the times when he'd appreciate her continued silence, so she gave it to him. Besides, she didn't think she could have spoken if he'd paid her to, not with the warmth of his body heating her back from shoulders to hips, with the weight of his arm lying across her upper chest, his elbow heavy between her breasts. She felt pleasantly trapped, not only by his embrace, but by her own desire to relax into it, into his warmth, into the sensuality of body against body, woman next to man.

After a moment she brought her hand up and wrapped it around his wrist, enjoying the feel of his hair-roughened skin under her palm. She stroked out to his fingers, where they curled over the point of her shoulder, and heard him sigh, felt it in his chest, in the breath that fanned her cheek as she leaned her head on his shoulder. She stood very still then, her fingertips resting on the back of his hand, absorbing all the wondrous sensations that flooded through her.

She knew she should move, knew she should try to stop whatever was happening, but she was wrapped up in something she couldn't control, enmeshed in a powerful net that bound her to him. Desire made a deep, hot pool inside her, weakened her knees, confused her breathing. As if in response, he squeezed her shoulder, tracing its shape with his fingers.

He drew in a ragged breath, then curved his palm up under her chin, turning her face to his. "Tracy . . ."

The softness of his whisper, the light in his eyes, told her he shared her desire even before his free hand splayed across her abdomen, pressing her back even tighter to him, against his arousal. His lips stroked over the corner of her mouth. She felt hers tremble apart through no doing of her conscious mind, felt her tongue flick out, seeking the taste of him. With a groan he half turned her and kissed her fully, widening her mouth with the force of his need.

His tongue slid between her lips, over her tongue, and she stroked it with hers. He tasted sweet, of chocolate—and of Don. He nibbled her lower lip, stroked her upper one, then delved deep again.

She murmured. He answered in kind. She sucked gently on his tongue, and he shuddered with pleasure.

His hand grew hot on her throat, the fingers spreading and sliding down inside the neck of her T-shirt, the tip of one caressing the upper curve of her breast.

A sound like a sob escaped her. Her head swam. Her knees went weak. She made another inarticulate sound and clamped her hand over his, holding it still. Holding it, but not moving it away. It felt too good there—too right. Her abdomen clenched as shafts of something akin to pain shot through her.

He removed his hand a moment later, and took his mouth from hers, trailed a line of hot kisses down her neck, then back up and nuzzled her earlobe. She released a tremulous breath, which he caught in his mouth as his lips took hers again, drawing deeply from her, plumbing her depths with a strong and evocative thrust and retreat that made her body surge in rhythmic pulses.

Just when she thought she might collapse, he broke their kiss and turned her to fully face him. His hands curved around her buttocks, lifting her to him. Breathing hard, they clung together, Tracy's fists clutching the front of his open jacket, her back pressed against the cool metal rail of the ferry's deck, until a male voice from a loudspeaker overhead burst them apart.

"It's time to land," Tracy said unnecessarily.

Don sighed and laughed on the same breath. "I think I'm too high up ever to come down again," he murmured.

There was nothing she could say. She was afraid she was too, and wondered how she was going to stop what was happening to her.

But stop it she must.

They spoke little on the rest of the trip home, but as they ascended the ramp from the wharf, Don took

Tracy's hand. "I think we need to talk about it," he said.

"I don't," she returned as she slipped away and evaded his grasp. He noticed she didn't try to pretend not to know what he meant.

She'd been dodging not only his touch, but his efforts at conversation ever since they'd left the upper deck of the ferry. Conversation of the sort he'd wanted had been impossible, of course, while they were in the mob of people returning to the car deck and debarking with the other foot passengers. There were still too many people around as they made the short walk to where he had left the car. Once inside the car, he'd thought they might take a few minutes to assess what had hit them both, but she'd made it impossible by keeping up a steady commentary on the history of Malcolm Island and its Finnish settlers.

Then, when the road deteriorated to little more than a track, and he had to concentrate on keeping the car out of the ditch, she'd fallen silent. With her slumped in the corner, her breathing steady, and her eyes closed, he'd thought she was asleep, however unlikely that seemed, with the rugged track bouncing them from rut to rut. When he'd parked near the dock, he'd found she was no closer to sleep than he was. She all but bounded out of the car.

She was in the Zodiac, with the motor fired up and the lines untied before he finished hauling his flight bag out of the trunk and locking up the car. The contents of the smaller bag he'd brought with him the first day were depleted.

The noise of the powerful outboard and the slapping of the Zodiac's hull on the choppy seas had precluded the kind of talk he'd had in mind.

But now there were no people, no rough road, and no outboard engine roaring in his ear. There was only an incredible array of stars overhead, a huge, clear moon, brighter than any he'd seen in years, and the faint lap of water against the rocks and pilings.

Just that, and him, and Tracy.

Just what he wanted. All of that and— Ease up, he reminded himself as he caught up to her and strode along at her side. "Slow down. Let's talk, Tracy."

"No," she said. "It's late. We both need sleep."

He caught her hand and drew her to a halt. "It's barely eleven o'clock," he said, "and what's happening between us is too important simply to ignore."

She took two more steps, and he saw her shoulders square up as if she were gearing herself for a battle. She stopped, turned, and faced him. "*Nothing* is happening between us," she said, her tone firm, her expression unreadable. She sounded so certain, he had to wonder if she really believed it.

He shook his head. Tracy Maxwell was anything but stupid. She knew as well as he did that they'd lit a fire that wasn't going to go out simply because she said so.

"Sweetheart, I beg to differ."

She smiled tautly. "You can beg for anything you want," she said, and swung away from him. "However, you won't get it any more than I got what I wanted one time when I begged."

This time he managed to capture her hand and pull her around to face him. "What? Is this all because you're still sore at me for resisting you fifteen years ago?" He wondered if she'd had the faintest inkling of what it had cost him to send her away.

"No." Tracy shook her head and stopped trying to get away. "No, of course not. It's just that . . . the whole idea of . . . of you and me is, well, ludicrous, Don."

"Ludicrous how?"

"Face it, whatever I might have started fifteen years ago was started by a kid who didn't know what she was doing. But now I take responsibility for my actions. I've learned a bit of discretion, if nothing else. I don't take up with strangers."

"Strangers!"

"We're strangers. We don't know each other now. Our lives, our interests, our . . . focuses aren't the same. We don't even live in the same country."

"That's geography."

"It's still a fact of life."

"So," he reminded her quietly, "is sex."

"Exactly. What we experienced on the ferry was only that—sex. It may have started as sort of an echo from earlier days, but it went further than I intended to let it. It had more to do with your needing distraction from your worries about your son, and my having had a glass of wine with dinner, than it did with anything else. It blew in on the breeze like a tantalizing aroma that reminded us of something from long ago, but it's gone now. Done with."

"Some breeze," he said. "If it blew in on anything, it was a damned typhoon. And it's done with just like a typhoon when it's gone. They leave signs that they've been in town, Tracy, wreckage, and I feel as if one has just blown off my roof."

He stepped closer. "That storm started blowing fifteen years ago, Tracy, and it hasn't run its course yet."

She laughed, a light, genuinely amused sound that he might have bought if it hadn't been for the wild light he saw in her eyes. "I see. It seems I raised some . . . expectations in you that you could take a raincheck *then* and end up in my bed *now*. I guess I owe you another apology, because maybe those expectations weren't entirely unjustified, considering my actions. Then or now."

"Your current responses to me have no more to do with a long-ago girlish crush than my wanting you tonight has to do with a raincheck," he said. "Which, for your information, I did not see myself as seeking. When I said no to you then, it was an unequivocal no, without any kind of expectation that we might take it up again.

"This is about now, Tracy. Today. Tonight. Tomorrow. What's happening right now. I for one want to let it happen. Perhaps not tonight, if you need more time to be sure, but I fully believe it is going to happen. And when it does," he added with quiet adamancy, "it's going to be very, very good."

Heat rushed through her at his words. "And I for another," she said, "don't need any more time. I've decided already, and the answer is no—today, tonight, and tomorrow." Oh, damn that tremor in her voice. "Please understand. I have no time for romance."

He frowned and touched her lips, tracing their shape. At once she put a smile on them, lest he see somehow into the sadness of her heart. "Everybody has time for romance," he said. "When it happens, it happens, whether you like it or not."

He pulled in a long breath and released it slowly, studying her face as if trying to think of what to say to convince her. She was glad he couldn't see into her heart. If he could, he'd know she didn't need convincing that he was right in saying that something was happening between them. She realized it all too well.

"All I know," he said, "is that on the ferry we started something that not only felt damn good to me physically, it felt right . . . in here." He tapped his chest. "You kissed me, and I felt as if a light had gone on inside me."

She looked astounded. "*I* kissed *you*?"

He held her gaze. "We kissed each other," he said softly, and continued to lock gazes with her until she nodded—reluctantly. Fine. At least he had her agreement on that. He was on a roll. "And those feelings we generated in each other are worth some time on both our parts."

He saw the denial in her eyes before she voiced it. "Those feelings we generated have nowhere to go."

Don dropped the flight bag and closed his hand around her upper arm. "Do you need a reminder of exactly what happened," he asked, "and exactly where those feelings were leading?"

"No!" The sharpness in her tone told him a lot, but he knew she wasn't yet ready to give in to them, or to him. She stared down at his right hand until he let her go, though he'd been careful to keep his clasp gentle.

"All right," she conceded, looking up. "Something did happen. I've already admitted that. It was pleasant. We both enjoyed it. But it had nothing to do with reality."

He let out an explosive breath any broaching whale would have been proud of. It was all he could do not to drag her against him one more time. His hardness was a reality he couldn't ignore. He didn't think she'd be able to either, not for long. But when a lady says no . . .

Picking up his flight bag, he accompanied her onto the back porch.

At the door she turned back to him. "Good night, Don. Would you like a flashlight, or is the moon enough to light your way to your cabin?"

He glanced over his shoulder at the cabin with its small covered porch, and was suddenly swept with the potent memory of another moonlit night. He closed his eyes for a second, recalling the numbing terror, the moments of indecision while he wondered what to do with his unexpected armful of satin-clad girl. Pull her inside and risk losing control, or keep her on the doorstep while he argued her out of her plan—and risk having her parents see her there like that?

"I'll find my way," he said.

"Sleep well," Tracy said. "I'll call you, of course, if I hear anything from or about Eric. Good night, Don," she said again as she turned.

He almost let her go. He almost decided to leave things as they were until the next day, but as she turned, the moonlight slid across her face and he saw that her smile had gone. The bleak loneliness in her expression spoke directly to a similar emotion that had long lain dark over his soul.

Which was the lie, her seductive, wanton kisses, the need he felt in her, or her insistence that she had no time for romance?

"Ah, Tracy . . ." he said softly as he fit his hand around her nape and drew her toward him, running a thumb over the silken curve of her cheek, over the sad droop of her mouth. "Not like that," he murmured. "I can't leave you looking like that."

She turned that damned smile on again, as if it were a lamp she controlled with a switch. "Like what?" she said, but it was too late. He'd seen it, that deep, steady pain in her eyes.

"Alone," he said, then lowered his head and kissed her.

Tracy wished afterward that he'd been aggressive, made some kind of demand, or even been a little bit rough. That, she might have withstood. If he'd given her something to get mad at, she might have fought.

But his tenderness shattered her, made her tremble, brought an uncontrollable sob up from her chest, a heated rush of tears to her eyes. He cupped his hands around her face and brushed his mouth across hers. He didn't take, he gave. He held her loosely, kissed her gently, then lifted his head and gazed at her. "Please," he said. "Let me help you, Tracy."

"How can you?" she whispered. She ignored the tears she knew he must be able to see at the base of her lashes, hoping that he'd do the same. "This is something I must do alone."

"No," he said. "You never have to be alone, you never again have to carry alone the load you're carrying—unless you choose to. That's all I'm offering you. A choice. I'm here if you need me, Tracy. I want to be here for you."

To her dismay, the tears spurted out, and she squeezed her eyes shut to block others, but they broke free and splashed from between her lids, so unexpected and hot, she had no way of stopping them. "Oh, Lord, don't do that!" he said in a pained whisper. "Tracy, please, baby! God, I didn't mean to make you cry."

He wrapped her in an embrace so warm and filled with such comfort, she could only lean into it, slide her arms around his middle, and struggle against a grinding need to let herself weep in earnest. She, who hadn't wept in years. Not when she buried her mother. Not when the diagnosis was made regarding her father's illness, not when she comforted her little sister at the breakup of her marriage.

But now . . . now, when she needed more than ever to draw on those deep wells of strength she'd discovered within, they deserted her and another huge sob welled up and rolled forth, followed by several more.

She struggled for control, but it was lost. All that glued her together was Don's embrace as he continued to hold her without pressure, without demand. He stroked her back and let her cry until she was done.

"Better now?" he whispered against her temple presently.

"I'm sorry," she said. "You've got enough worries of your own. You don't need mine added to them."

"It's all right. You asked me to believe that nothing bad was going happen to Eric. Now I'm asking you to do the same. Nothing bad is going to happen between you and me either, Tracy, if that's what's upsetting you. I promise."

She lifted her head and leaned back against the steadying circle of his arms, making no attempt to hide her swollen eyes, her red nose. "Why?" she said. "Why did you have to come back?"

He smiled and wiped her face with the heel of one hand. "Why?" he asked as if it were a question he hadn't fully considered until that moment. "I guess . . . I think maybe I had to come back for you, Tracy."

Then, with one more soft kiss, he released her, hefted his bag, and strode away toward his cabin.

Tracy wiped her face with the sleeves of her jacket and watched him go.

EIGHT

It was the moonlight keeping her awake. That, and the faint, infrequent sounds of whales blowing as they passed by. Tracy arose, monitored several of the recorders, made a few notes, then slipped into a pair of thongs and wandered outside. The offshore breeze was cool, and heavy clouds piled themselves on the mountains of Vancouver Island, threatening rain by morning, unless the wind changed. For now, though, the moon shone on them, silvering their tops, glinting off the dark water, glimmering among the leaves of trees.

She very carefully did not look in the direction of Don's cabin. Reaching back inside, she unhooked a heavy flannel shirt from the row of pegs near the back door. Pulling it on over her nightgown, she ghosted down the steps to the path, hearing the crushed shells crunch lightly underfoot. At the head of the wharf she sat and propped her elbows on her knees, gazing out over the water, watching for the wisps of steam that should follow each blow. When they came, they were distant, nearly invisible.

All of that—the whales, her research, even her father—seemed far away. She had much more immediate problems.

Such as, what was she going to do about Don Jacobs and the way he affected her? She'd been kidding herself, trying to pretend that she needed time to get everything straight in her mind, that she couldn't make love with him without some kind of personal commitment. She also thought she'd been wasting her time trying to convince him she had no time for romance. He was right; when it happened, it happened.

Whether she liked it or not, she'd already made a commitment. She didn't know yet how deep it went, or how long it might last, but it was certainly there, if commitment equated willingness to try to find solutions to insoluble problems. She could almost feel the tip of his finger tapping her chest, hear his voice saying softly, "And here."

She knew all too well that a man could fool himself into thinking that he felt some kind of emotional involvement when his blood ran hot and his sexual needs were aroused. Of course, so could a woman, and experience told her to exercise caution before she placed her heart in any man's care again.

But was what she felt love? She didn't know. It was too soon to go around putting labels on it, yet he was the man she wanted. The only man, she now suspected, that she had ever really felt deeply about.

Yes, she'd been about to marry Will, and would have had he not jilted her. But would it have been the right marriage for her? Would she have ended up like Edie, a bride at twenty-one, a divorcee at twenty-two? Maybe Will had sensed in some way she hadn't that it wasn't going to work between them. Maybe he'd done her a big favor with his cowardly act of running off on their wedding day. Certainly, being single gave her the freedom to do what she wanted with her life.

She stood and walked back toward the house, changed her mind, and went into the garden at the rear, feeling restless, edgy, dissatisfied. Whom was she trying to kid? She was not free to do what she wanted with her life. Her life was on hold and there were times when, as hard as she tried not to, she resented that. Mostly, though, she managed to forget about it and accept things as they were.

It was telling Don about it that had brought the rage and frustration all so close to the surface.

If he'd never come, she'd still be going along in her quiet little rut, more or less at peace with herself.

Was he at peace, or was he lying on his bed, staring at the ceiling, alone in the dark night, worrying about his son? It must be almost impossible for Don to lie and wait for news, as difficult and as painful as it was for her to imagine him so.

She rose, stood irresolute for a moment, then clenched her fists and walked quickly back into the house. Moments later she slipped outside again, heading directly and without hesitation to his cabin.

All was in darkness. Maybe he *was* sleeping. Maybe

men didn't spend the night hours filled with dread as women did. Maybe he was able to put bad thoughts away and escape into sleep.

And maybe not.

She tiptoed onto the small porch and lifted her hand to rap on his door, then snatched it back. What in the world was she doing? Had she convinced herself he was suffering simply to justify to herself her own need to be with him?

She did want to be with him. She did want to hold him if he needed her, as he'd held her. What had he said? *I want to be here for you.* He wanted to help her carry the load.

Yes. And that's what she wanted to say to him, to do for him.

She lifted her hand again, and this time she knocked.

She also wanted, quite desperately, to go to bed with him.

Don stood in the window and watched Tracy emerge from the house. His heart went still, then slammed into his ribs as joy, elation, hope, soared through him, only to drain away as she turned without so much as a glance in his direction. She sat for a time gazing out over the water. He wondered what she was thinking about, why she couldn't sleep. He hoped her thoughts were more pleasant than his.

When she returned to the house but didn't enter, wandering along like a lost waif until she disappeared around the corner toward her mother's garden, he considered going to her. Was she grieving? Was that what her tears had been all about earlier? Did she go to the garden, where she might feel her mother's presence, when she was down?

He thought about his own pain and groaned. God, what if Eric *hadn't* followed him? What if he'd been taken by someone? Wouldn't there have been a ransom demand by now? He was by no means a rich man, but he'd get the money somehow, somewhere. Wouldn't Muriel have called if there'd been news? Maybe not. She wasn't above making him suffer. The woman had not a grain of compassion in her soul.

He remembered the softness of Tracy's lips, the comfort of her kiss, her soft-voiced conviction that Eric would make it. Why couldn't he hold on to that, lie down, and sleep? Lord, he needed sleep!

He sat in the one easy chair the cabin offered, shoving his legs out in front of him. He should go to bed, but he'd tried that. Every time he closed his eyes, though, despite his exhaustion, the darkness somehow triggered his imagination.

If he could just lie down and tell himself that Eric was resting safely somewhere, enjoying a great adventure, completely unaware that he'd been reported missing, he'd surely sleep. If Eric knew his parents were aware that he wasn't where he was supposed to be, of course he'd call. He was a good kid. He'd never worry them this way on purpose.

So if he knew, he'd call.

If he could . . .

Don groaned again. It always came back to that. His mind simply couldn't leave it alone. He lifted his head from the back of the chair, then sat erect, alert, as he saw a shadowy shape flit up the steps to his porch.

He was on his feet and across the room in a couple of long strides, the doorknob clutched in his hand, before he knew he was going to move. He stood still, wondering if it had been wishful thinking conjuring up a ghost, or if she was really there. He listened, heard nothing. Then he stopped breathing and listened harder.

Go to bed, he told himself. She's not there. But would it hurt to open the door and look? Oh, God! What if there was news? What if it was so bad, she was standing out there girding herself against the pain of delivering it? What if . . .

He turned the knob, pulled the door toward himself, and Tracy nearly fell in.

He caught the hand she had raised to knock, held it balled into a fist inside his own, and stared at her, his arm rigid. She said nothing. He said nothing. He let her hand go and stepped back. Silently, she followed him. He swung the door shut, then turned her so the glow of moonlight through the window fell over her face.

"Someone called?" he asked, his voice an embarrassing croak filled with sixteen different emotions, none of which he could name.

He saw dismay flood her face. "No! Oh, no. I'm sorry. Of course you'd think that, my coming here and . . . I . . . couldn't sleep for wondering about you, worrying about you lying alone over here, thinking about Eric. That's why I, uh, came. And to bring you this." She gave him the cordless telephone from her kitchen. "This cabin's within range of the base unit. I didn't want you worrying that I might sleep through any calls."

He set the phone on the table. "I wouldn't have worried about that," he said, feeling guilty over the disappointment that welled up in him when he realized that had been her only reason for coming. He swallowed hard and looked into her eyes. The moonlight reflected from their shiny surfaces, turning them silver, unreadable. Why had he hoped for more? She'd already made her position clear. He'd already agreed with it.

"But you were worrying."

"I was thinking about Eric, yes," he said. "Every time I closed my eyes, pictures formed." *So I distracted myself by thinking about you.*

She touched his hand where it rested on the window frame. "Yes. It's hard, feeling helpless to fix things for someone you love when you can't . . . reach them."

He nodded. "Knowing he might need me, and that without knowing where he is I can't go to him, is probably one of the hardest things I've had to deal with."

"Want to talk about it?"

He shook his head and slid his hand around her nape, under her hair. "No. Talking wouldn't help. But . . ."

"But?" He heard the tremor in her voice, felt it in his hand on her neck. He didn't say anything, couldn't, could only look at her, all the while holding his mouth in a taut line, his shoulders so rigid they ached. She stepped closer, wrapped her arms around his middle, and rested her head on his shoulder. "But this will?" she asked.

"Yes," he whispered when he trusted his voice. He rested his cheek on her hair. "That's what I wanted. To hold you. To hold on to you."

"Everyone needs someone to hold on to now and then."

He turned, leaned on the wall, and drew her between his legs. "I didn't need 'someone' Tracy." His voice came low and ragged. "I needed you."

She stroked her hands up and down his back. "I'm here. I wanted to be here for you. You held me when I needed it. I wanted to return the favor." His arms tightened, and he tried to lighten things with a laugh before he cried from the sheer relief of not being alone to face the night and its terrors. "Boy," he said, "I sure hope Con doesn't find out about this."

"Nah." She laughed with him, shaking her head and leaning back enough to look up into his face. "Con's out like a light."

"Really?" he asked, and though Tracy couldn't see his expression in the shadows, she thought she heard a smile in his voice. "Did you slip her a mickey or bop her with a hammer?"

"Sorry," she murmured. "Trade secret. Besides," she went on, "Con knows I'm a big girl. I think she'd be more surprised that I didn't come to you than that I did. She probably expected me to do this Friday night."

His fingers flexed on her waist. She sensed that he frowned. "Why would she expect that?"

"Because she knew how I felt all those years ago."

She saw the light glint on his pupils as his eyes widened. "She did? And your parents?" There was horror in his tone.

"My parents saw me as a child. Con knew I wasn't."

His breath escaped in a rush, fanning across her cheek, fluttering her hair. "Do you think she also knew it was as hard for me to keep my hands off you then as it is now?"

Tracy nodded. "Probably. Con's a very perceptive woman."

She hesitated, then admitted, "After you left that morning, she gave me holy hell for going to your cabin the night before 'dressed like a tart,' as she put it. She delivered a tongue-lashing that totally eclipsed yours and told me I should be ashamed of myself for trying to ruin the life of a good, decent man. After I got over hating you, and resenting the fact that you'd gotten married almost immediately instead of waiting for me to grow up, I was as ashamed as Con told me I should be. Maybe more."

He cupped her shoulders and said, "I got married so soon because I accepted the first good offer that was made to me, hoping I could somehow ease the burn that you'd initiated. That 'good, decent man,' Tracy, got a nice girl pregnant the day after he got home and lived to regret it bitterly."

Tracy squeezed her eyes shut in pain. "Then I'm doubly sorry. And even more ashamed."

"Oh, hell!" he said, dragging her tightly against him. "Did I sound as if I were blaming you? I was an adult and responsible for my own actions. I knew the risks and got pie-faced drunk and ignored them."

"But . . ."

"But nothing. I'd been stirred up by a girl before, you know; you weren't the first to leave me frustrated. I was reacting as much with anger at myself for having wanted you so badly as I was to anything else. I guess nowadays they call it striking out. I call it being a jerk.

"Muriel and I had known each other in college. We'd . . . roomed together for a year and then I'd sort of . . . drifted away from her. When I turned up at a beach party she was attending that night, we gravitated together because I was in a foul humor and she was raw from another broken relationship. It was easy to slip into old habits and . . . comfort each other.

"A month later she told me she was pregnant, so we got married. It didn't work out, and later we got divorced. End of story. And it had nothing to do with you. You were in no way to blame for any of it, and I ended up with a great kid I love one helluva lot."

"Still, I'm sorry you had to live through that kind of personal regret, and the turmoil and grief of seeing your marriage end."

He held her away and looked into her face. "Yes, I regretted the marriage, and yes, I was hurt by it, though not as much as she was. Its breakup was my fault. I never loved her, though I pretended to both of us that I did, and when she finally saw the truth, she found love elsewhere. I'd have preferred her to ask for a divorce first, then wait until we were apart, but that's not the way it worked out, so things got a little . . . acrimonious. Especially when the man she'd been seeing patched things up with his wife, and she was left out in the cold. She wanted me to forgive her. For Eric's sake."

"You, uh, wouldn't take her back?"

He shook his head. "Not even to be with Eric full-time. As I said, I didn't love her. And if I had, I think my pride was too wounded for reconciliation to work. I don't deal well with rejection, I guess, even by someone I didn't really want.

"And I have never regretted being Eric's father," he added. "I'm grateful to her for him."

"That must make up for a lot."

Don heard the wistfulness in her tone and thought briefly of the dork who'd jilted her. Had she wanted children with the guy? Did she want children now? He thought of her dream of educating the whole world to the fascination of whales and wondered if she saw herself having that as well as a family, or would fulfilling the dream be enough for her?

"Yeah," he said. "It does. I like watching all the different phases of Eric's growth and knowing I'm contributing to it. It makes me feel good about myself, as though I'm accomplishing something of great value."

He felt her smile against his cheek. "I'm glad for you that you have him," she said. He knew she meant it.

They stood in silence for some time, arms around each other, breathing softly, Tracy listening to Don's heartbeat, absorbing the warmth of his body through his clothing and hers. Tremors passed through her at irregular intervals. Heat began to build and spread inside her. His hands moved restlessly over her back, her shoulders, fingers filtering through the ends of her hair. She heard him sigh almost silently, was aware of his increased heart rate.

Tension, need, made her move restlessly within the cradle of his thighs. He caught his breath sharply, and she held very still, trying not to feel the hard ridge of his arousal, but so aware of it, she could scarcely draw breath. Her breasts ached. Her nipples tightened. She wondered if he could feel them. Her fingers flexed against his back and he murmured her name, hands flattening on her buttocks, pressing her tighter to him.

She sighed and rose up on her toes, driven by an irresistible compulsion to be closer to him, part of him.

Don ached with growing need. He threaded one hand into her hair and tilted her face up as he slid his free hand down the front of her thick flannel shirt. "I see—" he began, then had to start again after clearing his throat. "I see you didn't come to me tonight dressed like a tart."

She shook her head as she moved apart from him.

She wrapped her arms around herself, protectively, he thought. Yearning rose in him. "No, I didn't."

Where she stood, her face was in shadow. The moonbeams caught in the tips of her dark curls, imparting a silver halo. "No white satin," she added, then cleared *her* throat. "But . . . but my intentions are the same as if I had."

Was that a hint of challenge in her tone, perhaps an element of defiance—or simply bravado to cover fear of rebuff?

He stayed with his back pressed to the wall, his palms splayed beside his hips. "Tracy?"

He saw her shrug. "Can't a woman change her mind?"

He let go of the wall, took a step toward her. "Oh, yes," he said. He touched her chin, her bottom lip. It trembled, and need shuddered through him. Emotions welled up in him, too new, too fragile to risk them by moving too quickly.

"Why did we waste all that time in idle chatter?" he asked. "You could have said something earlier, you know, instead of letting me go on and on about unimportant stuff."

"I guess . . . I guess because part of me thought you might throw me out again."

He stepped in close and took her hands, drawing her arms up around his neck.

"If you don't kiss me, I just might," he murmured against her lips.

He felt the softness of her laughter, tasted the minty sweetness of her breath. "Please don't," she said, and the tremor in her voice raised a lump in his throat. "I've learned over the years that I don't deal well with rejection either."

"A wasted lesson," he said, resting his hands on the curve of her waist, breathing in the scent of her hair. "You're not going to have to deal with it again. Not from me."

She sighed and leaned into him, parting her lips. He bent and took what she offered.

Her lips, the tip of her nose, were cool against his skin. The inside of her mouth was hot, so hot, so eager to meet his plunge that he used no finesse, exercised no technique, forgot there was such a thing. He simply needed to feel her mouth under his, feel her accepting him, feel her succumbing to the passion he could scarcely control.

Her tongue trembled against his as her body trembled in his arms. She strained to get closer. He strained to hold her tighter. It wasn't enough. It would never be enough. He felt the tension of her, the need in her, and it matched every similar emotion in him.

Don squeezed his eyes shut as he lifted her and sat in the easy chair, cradling her, moving his hands on her, feeling her shape, her warmth, her ragged breathing. He breathed deeply, trying to steady himself, trying to slow things down but unable to release Tracy, unable to resist her and wondering why part of him still felt he must.

She was an adult now, and she had come to him. She wanted him. Her kisses on every part of his skin she could easily reach, her whispers, inarticulate as they were, would have told him that had he not already known. She pulled his head down, and he met her seeking mouth, returned her kisses greedily until his head spun in dizzy circles and he was so hard, he thought he would burst.

"Stop," he gasped, dragging his mouth from hers, flinging his head back, all the while pressing her to him, moving her against him, unable not to. Her lips stroked his neck, his upper chest in the V of his shirt, her breath warm on his skin. "Slowly, baby. Savor it with me."

Cradled by his arm, she half lay across his lap, her legs over the arm of the chair. One of her hands rested on his waist, just above the top of his low-slung jeans. Her other hand curved around the side of his face, tracing the shape of his jaw. He heard the rasp of his whiskers.

Oh, God! He'd shaved . . . when? Early that morning, and not since. He was a mess. He wasn't ready for this. He wasn't prepared to— His back and shoulders went rigid.

He wasn't prepared!

She kissed him again, missing his mouth as he turned to bury his face in her hair. Her lips felt as incredible on the skin under his chin as they had on his lips.

"Tracy!" he pleaded, standing, tumbling her off his lap and steadying her as she found her feet. "Stop."

"Hmm?" She clung to him and toyed with the hair at the top of his chest, her mouth seeking his. "I'm just . . . savoring."

He couldn't resist the sweet tugging of her lips, the taste of her, the heat. He made a sound, a moan of frustration, and submitted for long, mind-numbing moments, then broke free. "Tracy, sweetheart, please don't! Listen to me. I don't have any way to protect you.

"I didn't," he said, trying to evade her kiss, "bring anything with me. I came to visit your father! I didn't come . . . come *equipped* to . . . do . . ."

She kissed him again, slow and deep, demanding and receiving his full participation. He couldn't breathe. He couldn't think. He could scarcely remain upright.

"That was shortsighted of you, wasn't it?" she murmured moments later, raking her nails down his chest inside his shirt.

"Hell and damnation!" he muttered, trying to extricate himself. She wasn't holding him, just gently touching his chest, yet he felt tethered by bonds of steel, the whisper of her hair across his hands as he continued to encircle her head with his fingers. "Yes, it was shortsighted." He groaned. "And stupid and . . . anything else you want to call it, but it's a fact, and it means we cannot, must not, continue, Tracy. I'm sorry, babe. I can't tell you how sorry!"

Why the hell hadn't he thought of it in Port McNeill? They'd walked right past a drugstore. *Twice.* And he'd hardly given it a second glance. He'd had other things on his mind. Oh, jeez! This was the worst kind of torture he could imagine. He caught her wrists and held her hands still, set her back from his turgid sex. He couldn't believe this! He was going to have to reject this woman twice in her lifetime, and he was afraid he'd never get another chance with her.

She struggled to free her right wrist from his clasp, and he had to let her go so she wouldn't hurt herself. He steeled himself, sure she was going to belt him one, but all she did was reach into the left breast pocket of that huge baggy shirt she wore and pull her hand out again, holding it palm-up before him.

In the shaft of moonlight he saw them. Three little foil packages. He stared, reached out a finger, and touched them to be sure they were real, stirred them around to be sure of the count.

"Three?" he half gasped, half laughed, folding weakly into the chair again, carrying her with him. "Sweetheart, I'm forty-one years old!"

She smiled a small, secret smile that only a woman knows how to smile and closed her fist over the packets. "We'll see," she said, and stood and walked away, leading the way into his bedroom.

He stood three feet away, his eyes glittering in the faint light, his shape large and dark. He appeared to be waiting for something, for her to do something, say something.

She stripped off her shirt and dropped it to the floor. He made a sound she couldn't interpret. She wished she had the guts to take off her nightgown as well, but suddenly her courage had deserted her. She couldn't bare herself to his scrutiny regardless of how little he'd be able to see, the moonbeams having failed to illuminate more than a corner of this side of the cabin.

Oh, Lord! Hadn't she done enough? Said enough? Hadn't she taken a giant step in his direction? Couldn't he at least meet her halfway?

Only hours before, he'd made it abundantly clear that he wanted her, but now that she was there, showing herself as more than just willing, he simply stood and stared at her. A strange sound rushed through her ears, blocking out even the hammering of her heart, yet the sensation that filled her was one closer to blindness than deafness. It allowed horrified thoughts to whirl unimpeded through her mind, shocking red on a black cloud.

Images of herself coming to him before, and then again tonight. Images of herself putting her arms around him. Images of herself reaching into her pocket and pulling out those condoms.

Had she been too aggressive?

Had his pushing her away and pleading lack of protection simply been a tactful way to get rid of her?

Had his undeniable physical response been an automatic one, one he'd rather have curbed?

She wanted to cry. She wanted to slink into the crack between the headboard and the wall. She wanted to magic herself out of there. She opened her mouth to say something, anything, but her lips were like dust, her throat was frozen, and her tongue stuck to the roof of her mouth.

It was then she realized he was shaking even harder than she was. He was shaking so hard, she could actually see his knees vibrating. The sound she heard was his breath whistling in and out, much too fast.

"Don . . ." She held out her hand to him. It was the same hand that held the condoms she'd brought. She laughed jaggedly and turned to toss them onto the nightstand. When she turned back, he was there beside her, his face half lit, his eyes bleak, his brows drawn down.

"Oh, God," he said, still not touching her. "I've never been so scared in all my life."

She tilted her head back to look up at him. "Why?"

"Why? Because you . . . because you're *you.* Because I want to . . . perform perfectly for you, to give you the best I am, the best I can be, but I want you so badly, all I can think of is the . . . is the . . . humiliation of premature ejaculation. I—oh, hell, I can't believe I *said* that!"

He ran a hand through his hair, the action tossing gaunt shadows across his face and setting the pale hair of his wrist aglow.

"Dammit, Tracy, I'm not twenty-six anymore!"

She stared at him. "And I'm not sixteen. Or twenty-six either. I'm nearly thirty-one to your forty-one, and as two mature adults, I think we're going to have to find some way to get past this mutual weirdness of ours."

"Mutual?"

"Oh, yes. You want me. Yet you stand there scared you won't be good enough to please me. I want you, and I stand here thinking you don't really like me because I'm too aggressive, bringing condoms to your room."

He opened his mouth to say something, but she planted her fists on her hips and demanded, "So? What are we going to do about it?"

Suddenly, he shouted with laughter. He caught her up in his arms, spun her around in a circle, then dumped her into the middle of the bed. She was still bouncing as he knelt over her, straddling her hips, cradling her face in his big, warm hands. "I'll show you what we're going to do about it," he said, and bent to take her lips in a soul-baring kiss.

Her mouth flowered open for him, her tongue met his thrusts, returned them. She raked her hands over his back and around to the loosely hanging front of his shirt. "And I'll show you," he said, lifting his head briefly, "what an aggressive woman does to me when her name is Tracy Maxwell."

While he nuzzled her neck and nipped the tips of her shoulders, she finished unbuttoning his shirt and threaded her fingers into the hair on his chest. He stiffened as she scraped her thumbnails over his nipples, then sat erect on her legs when she pressed her palms to the rigid muscles of his belly.

"You can do better than that," he whispered.

It took her a moment to open her eyes. "What?" In her bemused state she couldn't begin to guess what he meant.

She saw his teeth glint as he smiled. "I want you aggressive. Touch me, Tracy. Enjoy me the same way I mean to enjoy you."

She sucked in a deep breath and fumbled with his belt buckle. His waistband unsnapped on its own, the zipper sliding halfway until it was stopped by the bulge of his sex. She slid her hands around his lower back, inside his jeans, to the elastic of his bikini briefs, loving the silky feel of his skin, the power of his muscles under her hands as she glided them lower over his buttocks.

His breath rasped in and then out again, on a long "Yesss . . ." and she curled her fingers so her nails bit gently into his skin.

He leaned over her again, shoving aside the thin strap of her nightgown, his whiskers abrading her skin as he traced the upper rise of her breasts. She arched up to him, moaning softly, and he slid both straps down her arms. She pulled free of them, and his mouth drew one of her breasts inside, hot and wet and strong. She cried out and fell back on the pillow, cradling his face while he suckled.

He shifted, crowding one knee between hers, parting her legs, shoving her nightgown up from the bottom until it was little more than a strip of fine cotton bunched at her waist. His hands played over her, his fingers sure and strong, his touch creating exquisite pleasure. His mouth followed, leaving her gasping with the heat of its passage.

She tore his shirt from his shoulders, down his arms, and he shrugged out of it. "Lie on me," she murmured, then moaned a soft, sobbing little sound as his chest compressed her breasts. "Oh, God . . .

Don! I can't stand it!" she said, sliding her legs against the fabric of his jeans. "I need you!"

She burned. She pulsed deep inside, all hot and liquid and yearning. He rolled to his side, raked his nails down her stomach, then slid two fingers into the moist curls between her legs. She rose up to meet him, her head tossing from side to side as he glided through the slick wetness there. "Oh, hurry, please hurry . . ." she begged, but he did not.

With his hand stroking her to ever higher planes of ecstasy, and his mouth tugging at her breast, Tracy knew she was within seconds of climaxing. As if he knew, he slowed the rate of her ascent, bringing her down to a more bearable level of delight.

When her breathing was almost under control, she heard the rasp of his zipper, and as his hardness sprang free, she wrapped her hand around him, squeezing gently, loving the sensation of velvet-wrapped steel, cupping him with her other hand. His breath caught on a sharp gasp, then released in a groan of pleasure. She sat up, tilting him onto his back, and bent over his chest, her mouth finding a nipple, her teeth nipping at it. It puckered and hardened against her tongue, while his shaft pulsed within her clasp.

Then, clamping his hand over hers, he held it still and laid her down again, leaning over her to reach across to the nightstand. With his teeth he tore open the condom packet, and Tracy pulled her hand free to help him.

"Come here," he murmured, drawing her into his arms, rolling until his full length lay atop hers. He took the weight of his upper body on his elbows, his hands around her head, and plundered her mouth again. She parted her legs, cradling him, stroking his back, his buttocks, his hips, and they began to thrust in an instinctive motion. She raised hers against the weight of him, shifted slightly, and took him to her.

"Slowly, sweetheart," he said, but as she opened for him, lifting up again, digging in with her nails, slow was not what either wanted. With a groan he entered fully into her. With a cry of gladness she welcomed him.

He pulled back, then thrust again, deeper, lifting her higher. She rocked her hips, meeting his thrusts, clinging to him. Together they created a rhythm that caught them both, carried them out of themselves, took them soaring away until everything that she was, everything that he was or had been, metamorphosed and then coalesced into one bright point of light. It shattered, spilled out, and fell glittering down over them like silent diamonds in the night.

NINE

Tracy laughed softly against Don's shoulder. She lifted one hand and let it fall back down on his chest. "I'm a dishrag," she said.

He turned his head toward her. "We playin' charades, or what?" His voice was as slurred as hers as he fought the bonds of sleep.

She tried to raise her head, but her muscles refused to cooperate. "What, I guess," she murmured. "But I was thinking, what with you being afraid of Con and all, maybe I should go back to my own bed sometime soon, like in the next three seconds, before I fall asleep."

He chuckled and kissed her earlobe. "No, don't," she said. "Help me out of here, push me away or something."

He rolled toward her and draped an arm across her waist. "See? I'm helping you. I'm shoving you out of bed. But I'm a dishrag too, and we don't push real good."

Tracy snuggled close. "Mmm-hmm . . . other talents."

She came half awake when she felt him move apart from her, tried to open her eyes when she heard him bump into the dresser, then heard the bathroom door close. She tried hard to make herself ready to be up and capable of telling him good-bye when he came back to bed, but the effort was too great. She'd do it in just a minute.

When she felt him lift her hips and slide her twisted nightgown off her, she managed to open her eyes and make some kind of sound. He stroked her eyes shut with the tips of his fingers, and said, "Shhh . . ." When he climbed in beside her and pulled the sheet up over them both, she could only sigh and succumb.

What was she supposed to do once he had weighted her down with an arm and a leg? She had no strength to fight him off.

The ovenlike heat of his body seemed to surround her, and Tracy lost the last vestiges of consciousness.

Don followed her in seconds, but awoke first, momentarily disoriented until he inhaled and smelled Tracy's hair. He smiled, breathed deeply of the scent, and nearly dropped off again, but somewhere outside, a bird blew reveille.

He opened his eyes as memory flooded back. He sat erect. Eric! The phone, now on the bedside table, had not rung during the night. No news, he told himself, was good news. And it would ring soon. He stared at it, willing it to do so. It must. It was a new day. Lucky Tuesday. The day Eric would be found.

He sat with his back against the cool wood of the headboard, focusing on the thought of Eric reaching for a phone, Eric punching in the number of BIO Research, which Don had given him before he left; he never went anywhere without making sure Eric could reach him easily. He formed a picture of the phone ringing, of himself picking it up and answering, concentrated until he had it firmly embedded in his mind. It would happen. It would.

Beside him, Tracy stirred and squeezed her eyes shut as a sunbeam sliced through the gap between the curtains, angling across her face. Without waking, she moved her head so it didn't shine directly across her lids, and lay spread-eagle on her back. The sun cast a shapely shadow, the curve of a breast and shoulder, on Don's leg. Her hand, still dishrag limp, flopped across his lower abdomen, neatly excising worrisome thoughts.

Sliding back down in the bed, he lifted her hand, repositioning it. She turned from him onto her side, the sheet crumpled in the indentation of her waist. He trailed his fingers beneath it, along the graceful curve of her hip, spending long, pleasurable moments reliving events of the night before: her sweet, seeking touches, her giving generosity, her tightness and heat, the way she'd responded, rippling around him.

He wanted her again badly. He sighed.

Really to save her any embarrassment regardless of

the bold face she'd put on her decision to come to him in the night, Don knew he had to wake her up and see she got home before Con was up and around.

He would too, in a minute . . .

He lay propped on a elbow beside her, watching her sleep, seeing her breasts rise and fall, seeing her breath puff out a wisp of hair lying across her nose. Would its tickling awake her? If he tickled her, would she wake up? Did she wake up grouchy or glad? He longed to learn the answer.

If she was grouchy, he'd bring her coffee, let her move back into her naturally good humor slowly. If she was as joyous as the morning chorus of birds outside the window, he'd tumble her in the tangled sheets and share that joy.

Tracy, warm and giving in the night, had been magic. Tracy in the morning would be magic plus. And why not?

She'd said Con was seldom up before nine, hadn't she? That left him two hours to get Tracy back to her own house and her own bed, in privacy. He could even take her back there now and . . . No. He wanted her to stay where she was.

Lord, she looked pretty in his bed.

Her hair spread across the pillow and tumbled around her face, affording him only a glimpse of a flushed cheek, a pouting lower lip, and the tip of her nose. She lay with her arms crossed protectively over her chest, hands clasping her upper arms.

He smiled, wondering how long those defenses of hers would last if he were to make a determined raid.

A dawn raid . . .

Edging close to her, he conducted a reconnaissance mission, sneaking exploratory fingers between her upper arm and her ribs. She let her arm fall loose and shifted back against his chest, wriggling her bottom against his groin. He couldn't suppress his response, but tried to ignore it as he let his fingers march on, up and around the rise of a firm, warm hill.

When his careful, circuitous path reached its summit, he discovered a sleeping sentry. He touched it and it awoke, coming erect to stand on guard. Satisfied, he left it there to take care of things, and took his time, exploring in a southerly direction, over the curve of her stomach, feeling muscles quiver and ripple under his gentle assault. So far, no serious defenses had been raised.

When he made a foray down her upper thigh, she stirred and straightened that leg. He straightened his to accommodate her movement, a breath hissing in sharply at the sensation of satin skin gliding over his, the play of her taut buttocks pressed to him.

He spread his hand over her pubis, not moving, simply . . . there, and felt her stir again, wriggling back against him, disturbing him mightily. But he smiled, because he knew he was disturbing her too, if only minimally.

So far. He meant to disturb her a whole lot more before too long.

Was he giving her an erotic dream?

He pressed gently, making small circular motions with the palm of his hand.

Her pelvis tilted and her breathing changed. He cupped his hand, sliding two fingers into the warmth between her legs. Her hips came forward, rising to meet his caress, then rotated back, creating a unique caress of their own, exactly where he didn't need to be touched at that moment. Yet he couldn't resist eliciting the same response from her again, couldn't resist any more than he could the urge to slowly edge back from her, to feel her body follow his to the center of the bed. He slid out of contact, except for that one cupping hand, and she flopped to her back, exactly as he'd hoped, her hair sliding off her nose and cheek to curl in a dark pool on her shoulder, several strands caught in her lashes.

Rising up on an elbow, he discovered that cunning little soldier still on duty, joined by another just like it on an adjoining hillock, equally alert. With those two ready to spread the alert, it was time to either take them out of action or get them on his side.

He bent and placed his mouth over one, and buried the other under his hand. At once he knew whose side they were on. Real little turncoats, those babies.

As Don's mouth fit hotly over the tip of her breast, Tracy couldn't contain a soft moan of pleasure, though she'd have liked to go on pretending to be asleep for a long, long time. This was the most enchanting way to be wakened.

She opened her eyes and saw a burnished gold head bent over her, felt the sorcery of his tugging mouth, his teasing tongue. She stroked a hand into his hair, feeling its texture crisp under her palm, yet silky between her fingers. She drew in a tremulous breath and traced the shape of his ear, the hard, blunt line of his lower jaw.

"Don . . ." she murmured, and his mouth pulled harder for a second. A deep shudder coursed through her, another little moan escaped. He lifted his head, his lips glistening moist, his eyes soft and smoky blue behind gold-tipped lashes. "Oh, sorry," he said. "Did I wake you? Shall I let you go back to sleep?"

"Don't stop on my account," she said, stretching and wriggling. "Not if you're enjoying yourself."

"Oh, I'm enjoying myself, all right." He glided a hand over her forehead to move the hair half obscuring her left eye and smiled at her, bending closer.

She planted a hand on his chin and held him back as she turned her head away. "No! You can't kiss me!"

He nuzzled the sensitive flesh under her ear. "Why not? Remember, that's the right way to say good morning."

"I've got breath worse than a whale's."

"Not here, you don't," he murmured, nibbling his way back down to her breast. He kissed her, sucked, then bit gently while she squirmed. "Lie still," he said. "You're spoiling my game."

Tracy grasped the headboard to pull herself half erect. "What game?"

He laid her back down. "I've been playing soldier." He explained in detail, with gestures and demonstrations, how he played soldier, finding secret paths from here to there, crawling carefully up hills, seeing what was at their tops. By the time he got to how he had suborned the first of the two sentries and brought it over to his camp, she was gasping for breath. He moved on to prove how easily the other one had fallen for his persuasion. "Mmm," he murmured, "no whale breath here either."

After several moments, during which she squirmed considerably more, he lifted his head and smiled.

"Anyway, even if you have whale breath—which I seriously doubt—remember, so do I."

She looked at him through the tangle of hair that covered her eye again. "You think we'd cancel each other out?"

"I think, after the first couple of seconds, neither one of us will notice."

To her amazement, he was right.

Moments later Tracy said, "Can girls play soldier too?"

He shook his head. "Not a chance. That's strictly a guy game."

She smiled. "Then maybe I'll play sailor instead."

Don grinned at her playful tone. "Yeah? How do you play sailor?"

She made a disgusting *ooo-gah, ooo-gah, ooo-gah* sound, said "Dive! Dive! Dive!" and took her submarine down under the covers. Don gasped, then groaned, and flopped onto his back, tossing the covers off in time to hear her murmur, "Oh . . . look at that! The enemy has risen. Man the torpedoes."

Don lifted his hand and let it fall limply to his chest. "I'm a dishrag," he said, looking sly and smug and totally satisfied.

Tracy grinned and sat up, ready to swing her legs off the bed. "Sure you are," she said. "Don't forget, I listened to that one once before, believed you, let down my guard, fell asleep—and look what happened."

He came up on his elbow, grabbing her, and pinned her back against the mattress, inserting one leg between hers. He kissed her two "guards" until they were back on duty, or maybe on his side, and said, "Hey, now, come on! That first time we were both dishrag limp, in case you aren't aware of it, was about six hours ago. I've had a good night's sleep since then, and a hell of a fantastic wake-up call. My dishrag status isn't likely to be as longterm this time. Hang around, kiddo, and I'll prove it to you."

"Oh-ho, so now we're up to 'proving' things, are we?" Tracy linked her hands behind his head and smiled. "I thought being forty-one was a problem for you." She made a *tsk* sound. "Premature ejaculation indeed!"

He blushed. She loved that. He *blushed.* He also buried his face between her breasts, his voice vibrating her bones, his breath steamy. "Jeez! Of all the dumb things to say. I guess I knew it was obvious I didn't have impotence to worry about, so I focused on the next worse thing." He raised his head. "And you quit laughing at me."

He moved insinuatingly against her, his eyes looking dark and mysterious, and she quit laughing. "Today," he said, "I feel twenty-six. Maybe even seventeen."

Tracy bent one knee and rubbed her inner thigh against his hip. "And today I feel sixteen."

He knelt between her legs and drew his hands down her body, his laughing face going suddenly serious. "Not to me you don't," he said, encircling her waist for a moment before his hands rose to cup her breasts. "To me you feel like the woman you thought you were then, and that I knew you would become in time." He leaned forward and kissed her mouth, then her breasts, then her stomach, as if in accolade. "The woman you are."

Tracy quivered. In his arms she had been transformed into that woman at last, the one she'd known she could become too, and had never been before.

She stroked her palms over his back, his waist, his lean hips, then drew them around until she had captured his manhood. He lifted up again, kneeling proudly over her, and let her stroke and admire him.

As she slid her gaze sideways at the nightstand, he smiled. "It's all right," he said. "There's one left."

"One left," she agreed, reaching for it and opening the package. Tenderly, with agonizing slowness, she rolled it onto him. "So long as you realize that's all there is between us and abstinence."

His chest rose and fell rapidly. "I think," he said raggedly, "that in very short order, I'm going to feel like I'm ninety-one, so it won't matter a whole bunch."

She smiled and drew him down to her. "Wanna bet?"

He kissed her deeply before lifting his head and saying, "Then I guess we're going to have to make another trip to Port McNeill." He closed his eyes and kissed her again. After that they both stopped talking.

Somewhere not far away, an orca exhaled, puffing a long, sibilant sound into the air. Tracy kissed Don's warm, man-scented shoulder, stroked the surprisingly soft growth of copper-colored whiskers on his chin. He smiled in his sleep.

Silently, she slipped out of bed and tiptoed from the room, pulling on her shirt as she went. She wasn't sure where her nightgown was, but it didn't matter. She could collect it later. Meantime, she had a job to do, and the day was slipping away minute by minute.

Besides, if she stayed, she'd probably wake Don up, and the longer he could sleep, the less time he'd have to worry about Eric before the boy turned up.

It took her less than ten minutes to shower and dress, and probably twice that to argue with Con about eating breakfast. She compromised on taking a lunch, which Con made and stuffed into a tote bag for her while she loaded the rest of her gear.

After a swift run across Johnstone Strait, she slowed to a crawl when she reached her objective. As a scientist at a recognized research center, she was authorized to enter the wildlife preserve. She lowered an anchor off the bow, and once it was firmly set, shut off the motor, swinging in silence with only the chuckle of ripples slapping under the flat bottom of the boat, tickling up against its sides.

The number of whales congregated told her the rubbing beaches were in use, but she stayed where she was so as not to disturb the animals.

Tracy's interest was in trying to learn if there were certain phrases used between whales leaving the beach, and others coming in to take their place.

With that in mind, she dropped a hydrophone over the side, tuning in on whatever conversations might be happening against the shore. There was little whale chatter, but she set the tape recorder and sat back, adrift in her own thoughts, her memories, the sweetness of the night before, contrasted to the bitter one preceding it. How could a person's life change so radically in the space of twenty-four hours?

But . . . despite what had happened between her and Don, had her life changed all that much? She had made no decisions, spoken of no commitments. And neither had he.

She still didn't even know what he might do about having the grant stopped. He was, first and foremost, a member of the board of directors of the Meteor Foundation with an allegiance to the other members and its sponsors. If he felt he couldn't morally change the status of the grant without lying to them, he wouldn't do it. And she wouldn't want it any other way.

It was that strong code of ethics she'd always known him to have, that very uprightness she had thought to capitalize on, when she first knew he was coming back. She knew it hadn't changed. Would she love him this much if it had?

She sat abruptly erect. *Love?* She hadn't wanted to let that word creep into her thoughts, lest it work its way into the fabric of her being.

Was she in love with him, or simply infatuated again? Had she ever been infatuated with him, or had her feelings for him, born in the innocence of girlhood, lain dormant and flared back to life at his return?

She shook her head. Deep inside she knew there was no question. She was in love with him. It did no good for her to tell herself that it was too soon, that it didn't happen like that in four days. It *did* happen because it *had* happened.

Now the question was, loving him, shouldn't she also be able to trust him? She heard the question, understood its import, but the answer didn't seem to be anywhere close.

And neither did the whales. While she had sat there, immersed in her thoughts, they had moved on, their vocalizations nothing more than a faint, eerie music that her less-than-modern hydrophone had difficulty hearing.

The breeze had begun to pick up by then, and the swell to increase even in the protected confines of Robson Bight. Strange, how easy it was to up anchor and head, not in search of the departed whales, but back home. To Don. And whatever the rest of the day might bring. And the night.

She had retrieved the camera they had planted in a

strategic location the previous day, hoping there would be some really spectacular footage on its film, when a thought struck her.

That's all there is between us and abstinence, she'd said, and it was true. Would Don have— No. He'd have needed to stay near the phone. He probably wouldn't even have thought about it. That meant it was up to her. She swallowed hard, shocked and disbelieving at the aversion she felt, the embarrassment she thought she should have long ago grown beyond. This was ridiculous. Of course she could do it. She was an adult. And so what if the town was small, the store smaller, and everyone knew her? She laughed at herself, cleared the entrance to Robson Bight, and put on speed.

She was surfing toward Sointula on a following sea when her call sign crackled through the static on the VHF radio.

"Hi, Tracy! That you heading northeast ahead of me?" the caller asked after they'd switched to a non-emergency band. She'd known Pete for years. He ran a whale-watching operation out of Telegraph Cove. She turned and saw one of his tour boats half a mile back, and confirmed her location relative to his.

"Got me a seasick kid here who says he's supposed to be meeting someone at your place," he went on. "You want to save me a trip?"

"My God!" she said. "Is his name Eric?" Even before she heard the affirmative reply, she'd swung her wheel hard over at full speed, oblivious of the spray sheeting in over the side as she turned back to meet the other boat.

Minutes later, Eric aboard, she put the Zodiac into low orbit and flew.

Eric . . . safe. Don held his son's rangy form tightly, feeling him shiver, feeling the quaking of the sobs Eric tried to suppress. "It's okay, son," he said, brushing his lips over Eric's too-warm forehead. "You're safe now. You're here. We're together." He didn't want to, but he had to ask, "Did anyone— Are you hurt? In any way?"

"No. Put me down. I can walk," Eric croaked, but Don noticed he didn't struggle, didn't try to insist.

"You're sick," he said.

Eric's head rolled against Don's shoulder. "Just seasick. That boat *never* stopped moving. Not even at night."

At night? Eric's response raised more questions than it answered. "You'll feel better soon," he said, but he had no way of knowing that was true. Eric's skin burned hot against Don's as he lowered his cheek to the boy's forehead. Where had he been? How long had he been ill? What else had happened to him? He didn't want to think about that. Whatever might have befallen his son, he was alive. The rest they could deal with later.

He followed Con inside the main house and into a bedroom, where she flipped the covers back so he could deposit Eric on the bed. Con tugged his jacket off him, then reached for the bottom of his sweatshirt, but he wrapped his arms around his chest. "You're not undressing me!"

"Hah! You think you got somethin' I ain't seen before?" Con asked, but she left him his dignity, only placed a hand across his forehead. "Lie down," she said. "You got a fever."

Don saw Eric's chin jut and pressed gently on his shoulder. "This is Con," he said. "Everyone around here does what she says, so you better too."

"He's got that right," Con said. "You listen to your pa. He's got sense enough to be scared of me."

Again Eric tried to sit up. "My dad's not scared of anyone," he said, "and neither am I."

"Of course you're not," Don said, pulling Eric's shoes off. His socks were damp; those went too, and he rubbed the boy's big, bony feet between his hands. "That's because you don't know Con. Trust me on this one, bud. You be scared of her. She means what she says."

Eric tried to laugh, but his eyes flooded and his chin trembled. He met Con's mock-fierce glare though, and refused to shed the tears. Suddenly she grinned at him and tousled his hair. "I'll get you some ginger ale, pal. That always tastes good when you've been pukin' your guts out."

Don nodded. "Thanks, Con. I think he could use that."

The minute she left, Eric stopped trying to be tough. "I'm so sorry, Dad," he said, sitting up and blubbering against Don's chest. "I just went crazy when Mom changed her mind like that at the last minute and said I couldn't come with you. I know it was stupid to run away. I know you're mad at me, but I didn't mean to scare everyone. I didn't think she'd even suspect I wasn't with the Coopers until after I was here. And then I thought you'd call her and make it okay."

"All right, now take it easy. I'm not mad. I might be later, but right now I'm just happy you're safe." He held Eric, rubbing his back the way he had when he was a little boy, until the worst of the weeping seemed over. He eased him back on the pillows, dragged his damp jeans off him, then pulled the covers up, using a corner of the sheet to wipe Eric's tears dry. Eric turned his face away in shame.

"We can talk about everything later," Don went on. "You just rest now. I'm going to stay right here beside you." He smoothed Eric's damp hair back from his forehead, then looked up as Con came in with a glass of ginger ale. He helped Eric sit and held it while the boy drank thirstily, then lay back down.

"Tracy called the doctor. He's on his way," Con said quietly.

"I don't need a doctor!" Eric wailed, sounding closer to four than fourteen.

Don soothed him as he silently blessed Tracy. She had all the right instincts. "Son, you're sick."

"Seasick. I told you. That boat never sat still, up and down, up and down, forever, and at night, when he shut me in that locker, it was awful!" He shoved Don's restraining hands back and struggled to sit up.

Shut him in a locker? Don stared at his son, hands clamping over his shoulders, but Eric shrugged him off.

"Gotta call Mom." He looked piteously at Don. "Dad, you gotta believe me! I didn't *know* until today she knew I wasn't camping. I didn't know the cops were looking for me, or that you guys were worried about me. I'd never had done that to you. Honest. Please, you gotta make her believe me. Oh, brother! She's gonna *kill* me!"

"Eric, I've already called her the second Tracy radioed Con that she had you aboard her boat. Trust me, your mother is not going to kill you. You lie down."

He could tell it was easier for Eric to give in, because he lay back without further argument and closed his eyes, his lashes black against his pasty skin. Don watched him swallow convulsively a few times, and suspected the room continued to rock as badly for him as the boat he'd been on. What boat? How long? With whom? And why had he been shut up in a locker?

The questions reeled through his mind as he watched Eric's face, saw him slip into a light doze. Where the hell was that doctor? How long would it take him to get there? How could civilized people live like this in isolation, the nearest hospital miles away and totally inaccessible other than by boat?

Eric moaned in his sleep and coughed, a deep, racking sound that rattled his ribs. Don divided his attention between his son and the empty stretch of water visible through the window. All the while, his ears strained to hear the sound of an approaching boat.

Instead, a floatplane circled the bay and landed. He watched as a uniformed RCMP officer stepped out onto the pontoon while Tracy held the wing, then the officer handed out a man with a black bag.

He saw Tracy bar the policeman's way, her fists on her hips, saw him move her aside to make way for the doctor, who jogged toward the house. Eric coughed again, and Don turned back to him.

"He's sick," Tracy said, stepping between the police officer and the ramp. "You can't arrest him. Besides, he's just a kid, border jumper or not."

"Take it easy, Ms. Maxwell." The policeman drew her aside so the doctor could pass. "I only want to talk to the boy. If anyone's in trouble—besides young Eric with his parents—it's the boater who brought him across the line, then dumped him off at Telegraph Cove. But believe me, I don't arrest kids unless I'm absolutely forced into it. So long as this one is safely in his father's care, we can probably look at his actions as an error in judgment. But I do need to speak to him."

Tracy nodded in reluctant agreement. The man was only doing his job.

He couldn't have been in the house two minutes when another plane landed in the bay, closely followed by a high-powered boat. Seconds later Tracy realized that someone else was in trouble, and that someone was her.

TEN

A man stepped onto the pontoon of the plane, camera on his shoulder, panning the dock area, the house. The plane taxied in, its pilot swinging wide to avoid the wing of the RCMP craft, and put his in on the other side of the dock, causing the cameraman to curse at the top of his lungs and scramble back inside. He appeared out the other back door, this time on the pontoon nearest the wharf, and jumped nimbly across the narrowing gap.

Tracy stood frozen, not knowing what to do, where to look, what to say. The pilot stepped out, reached back in and handed out a woman, who jumped just as nimbly as the cameraman, onto the dock.

"Tracy Maxwell?" she said, thrusting a microphone into Tracy's face. "Lorraine Winston, Channel—" The rest of what she said was lost to the roar of the speedboat making a highball approach to the wharf, but Tracy recognized her anyway. She was a stringer for one of the Victoria area TV stations, and often reported on doings on this end of Vancouver Island.

Out of the speedboat leapt a man and a woman, both with tape recorders, and another man with a notebook. He was large, bald, and bearded, moved slowly, and looked vaguely familiar to Tracy. He smiled, and she nodded, sure she knew him from somewhere.

"Where is the boy, Ms. Maxwell?" one of the newcomers demanded, leaning over Lorraine Winston's shoulder with a tape recorder. "How did he get across the border?" Someone else jumped in with another question: "How do you feel, knowing he ran away from home and traveled all that way just to visit the Johnstone Strait killer whales?"

Tracy's eyes felt as if they were being jerked back and forth on strings as she tried to discern who was saying what and direct her replies, none of which was ever allowed to be completed before another question was shouted into the fray.

"Do you think his action is directly attributable to the recent controversy about whales in captivity? You're on record as being opposed. Did you encourage him to run away in order to generate publicity for what you believe in?"

"Of course not!" she said, aghast that anyone might think so. "He . . . he didn't come to see the whales. He came to see his father, who is visiting here." That set them off on a different tack.

"His father is a director of the Meteor Foundation.

What was his reason for coming here? Is BIO Research in line for a grant?"

"He came for a private—"

The woman with the tape recorder elbowed the woman with the microphone, shouting, "Did Donald Jacobs arrange to have his son pretend to run away? Is this, in reality, a clever parental abduction? Does Jacobs plan to stay here with you? Is he going to fight for custody here? Does he intend to send the boy back to his mother, who has legal custody in the state of California?"

That set off another rapid clamor, and Tracy could scarcely make out one question over the others. "The police are here. . . . The boy is an illegal immigrant. . . . What have the RCMP said. . . . Will you and his father be arrested, too, for—"

"Stop it!" she shouted into the welter of voices. "I can't tell you anything! Please, just go away. I don't know anything that might interest you. Eric just arrived minutes ago. All I know is he's sick. I haven't spoken to his father since I brought Eric here. I haven't spoken to the police except to report Eric safe and sound. I can't answer your questions."

Oh, Lord! Why hadn't she waited until she got home to make her report over a secure landline? Even calling Con on the radiophone might have been enough to alert any news person listening for a mention of a missing boy, but calling the police had surely torn it.

"What's your involvement with Eric's father?" shouted a man who had crowded in front of Lorraine

Winston, forcing the cameraman to scramble to change positions. "Can you tell us what his reaction was to seeing his wife's tears on TV last night? Does he mean to go back to her?"

Lorraine neatly sidestepped him. "Get out of the lady's face, Larson," she said. "I was here first and it's the boy we're interested in, not his parents' private lives. Where has he been since early Friday morning, when he left home?" she asked, pushing the microphone toward Tracy again. "It couldn't have taken him until Tuesday to get here. Has he been with you and his father all along? Did he see his mother's heartfelt plea on TV for him to call her? Is that why he came forward when he did? Were his running away and then his so-called 'discovery' staged, as has been claimed, to draw media attention to BIO Research?"

"No! Of course not! I—"

"Then why the media blitz regarding his running away?"

"His father wanted him back and safe!"

"What about the rumors that he was trying to force his parents back together by running away? Can you tell us—"

Tracy shoved both her hands into her hair. "I thought you weren't interested in his parents' private lives!"

The man with the notebook, who had so far been quiet, merely jotting things down, stepped forward, shielding her with his bulky body, putting a fatherly hand on her back. He half turned, speaking over his shoulder in a plumy English accent. "You people are acting like jackals. Give the young lady a break. Let's ask our questions one at a time, and keep the tabloid issues to a minimum, if you please."

Then, still sheltering Tracy, he said quietly, "Take it easy, Ms. Maxwell. Remember me? George Fellowes. I did a three-page in-depth article on your father and his research perhaps eight years ago."

"I—yes. I remember."

He smiled, his eyes crinkling charmingly. "I'd like to ask you a few short questions, if you don't mind," he said, and she nodded, relieved to find somebody sane in this crazy house of reporters and their unbelievably impertinent questions.

He stepped aside so he was no longer blocking her from the camera's eye. "If you could just give us a brief statement, Ms. Maxwell, then we can be on our way and leave you in peace."

"What do you want to know?"

"Just tell us what you know," he said easily. "First, what brought Mr. Jacobs here?"

"Mr. Jacobs came for a private visit with my father," she said, trying to regain her cool. "He was on staff here one summer many years ago and hoped to renew his acquaintance with my father."

"I see. And where is your father?" asked George Fellowes. "As the head of BIO Research, a statement from him would be appropriate too."

"That won't be possible. My father is—"

"Why don't you let your father respond to that himself, Ms. Maxwell?" one of the others cut in, taking a step around the group and heading for the ramp.

Tracy grabbed his arm. "You can't go up there! My father isn't there anyway. He has no statement to make. He isn't even aware of any of this. He—"

"That's right. He's not aware of much of anything, is he?" George Fellowes asked, then consulted his notebook. "He's been maintaining an extremely low profile since he, er, left his position at IWU."

She stared at him. She'd thought he was a friend, but something in his unctuous manner began to worry her. "He's . . . away," she said, holding his gaze, searching it for anything untoward.

George smiled again, still kindly. "Away where, Ms. Maxwell? Is he back in the mental hospital where he was a patient for several months following your mother's death? Is the Meteor Foundation aware that he was let go by the university as a result of allegations of—"

"No!" Tracy backed away from him, feeling betrayed. "My father retired at over the age of seventy! He was not 'let go' for any reason at all, and I don't know what kind of allegations you might be talking about."

"Then tell us where he is," said George Fellowes in a reasonable tone, "and let us interview him for ourselves."

"I—no! My father is—"

"Professor Maxwell is in Alaska," said Don, sliding a strong arm around Tracy's shoulder. She concentrated on not letting her knees cave in from sheer relief. "I spoke to him myself not twenty minutes ago. He asked me to say this on his behalf: He is delighted to know that my son has been found, and even more delighted to know that he is safe. He's invited me to take Eric to visit him there, where he'll introduce him to some Alaskan orcas. We may do that next week."

"Are you Donald Jacobs? How is you son? How did he find his way to this remote island? Did you give him explicit instructions? Are you and his mother going to reconcile? Does she know you're visiting another woman? Do you—"

Don held up his hand, and to Tracy's amazement, the cacophony of questions came to an immediate halt.

"I am Don Jacobs, yes, and I'm prepared at this time to make a brief statement regarding my son if you'll all shut up and let me get on with it."

They stood without even blinking. In the silence, Tracy could hear the soft whir of the TV camera.

"Eric left San Diego early Friday morning," Don said in a flat tone. "He told his mother he was going camping with friends. He hitchhiked in stages to a point near the border in Washington State, where he realized he wouldn't get across the border by road. Following the advice of a trucker, he stowed away on a boat heading north out of Anacortes, Washington. When the skipper of that boat finally got around to reading the newspaper he bought in Campbell River this morning and saw a story about my son, he put him ashore in the first inhabited place he came to.

"Eric had no idea that his friends had returned early from camping, and therefore was not aware that his mother and I have known of his absence since yesterday. He was unaware that his name and description were so widely distributed. He is sorry for causing everyone such concern, and sorry for all the media attention his adventure has caused. It is my understanding that after he's been interviewed by the RCMP, he and I will be free to leave."

He stepped back, arm still around Tracy's shoulder. "That is all I have to say on the subject, and all Ms. Maxwell has to say."

He turned Tracy and began to walk away, but the voices and footsteps followed them. Don stopped and turned them both around again. "Tracy, do you want these people here?"

She said no in a voice she was ashamed of, it was so small and shaken.

"Then, ladies and gentlemen, I suggest you leave. If you don't, you'll be charged with trespass." He aimed a pointed look at the RCMP emblem on the tail of the plane.

Without a further word, he and Tracy left.

On the porch, out of sight of the dock, Tracy slumped against the wall, shaking so hard, she could scarcely stand. Don steadied her. "You okay?"

She nodded and leaned against him. "Thank you," she said. "That was . . . terrible. Why did he have to do that? Ask all those questions about Dad, I mean? It had nothing to do with anything and—"

"I know," he said, stroking her hair back from her face. "But people like that can sense when you're unwilling to discuss a certain subject. They zero in on it by instinct. If you don't want to talk about it, you must have something to hide."

She shuddered. "Is Eric okay? He had a fever. I—"

"He's okay." For an instant Don's arms tightened around her. "Look," he said reluctantly, "I have to get back in there, but if you can hold on for just—"

"I'm fine now," she interrupted, pulling herself erect, out of his arms, where she'd have preferred to remain burrowed. She smiled weakly. She could see how torn he was between her needs and his son's.

"Sure?" he asked, searching her face. "The officer wants to talk to him. I said he could, but not until I got back." He grinned wryly. "I left Con guarding him, and I don't want to leave that poor Mountie in peril any longer than I have to."

She managed another smile, hoping it felt more secure than it looked. "I'm fine. You go on in. I'll come inside in a minute. I just want to be sure they've gone."

As she spoke, they heard the seaplane roar, and the boat's engine adding its lower-toned rumble as the plane taxied out of the bay.

She closed her eyes and slumped onto a deck chair.

"Tracy?"

She looked up, waved a hand at him, and said, "Go, already!" With a frown, he did so.

Tracy was in a storage shed, putting away the equipment she'd used during the day, when Don appeared in the doorway half an hour later. She turned at the sound of his step, seeing him outlined against the glare of the setting sun, a dark figure, tall, broad-shouldered, his expression hidden in shadows.

Suddenly, her newly acknowledged love for him terrified her. It was so new, so fragile, like a shimmering glass bubble; it could too easily be broken. What if he didn't want it? What if he were there to tell her that now that Eric's interview with the police was over, he and Eric were on their way. What if he were about to say that it had been nice, and he was grateful to her for her comfort during his time of need, but now that he had his son back, he felt differently and had come to say good-bye.

She moved to the far side of a large wooden packing crate that was used as a work surface and laid out a diving suit she hadn't used that day. It needed no attention at all. She needed something to do with her hands.

"How's Eric doing?" she asked.

"He's going to be fine," he said, holding out a hand to her, a hand she sidestepped as she went about her work. "He's sleeping," Don continued, his gaze fixed on her. "How about you?"

She gave him a wide-eyed stare. "Am I *sleeping*?" She laughed. He did not.

"Tracy," he said, taking a slow step toward her. "What's wrong?"

She backed up, holding the suit between them. "Nothing," she said, and unhooked a hanger from a metal bar in a corner of the building. "Why is Eric running a temperature?" She slipped the wooden hanger into the suit. "Being seasick shouldn't make him feverish."

"He's dehydrated and has an ear infection that affected his center of balance," Don said in the same tone he'd used to quell the reporters. "That accounts for most of his symptoms of seasickness. He'd have felt that way on dry land. He's had an injection of Dramamine and one of penicillin, and should be feeling much better when he wakes up."

"Good," Tracy said, and finally hooked the hanger back over the rod. She carefully arranged the arms and legs of the suit until it hung just so.

"That means," Don continued, "that we'll need to stay around another couple of days."

"Of course," she said, trying to make her tone bright and cheerful, while inside her stomach lurched. A few more days? How could she live through them, knowing they might be all she'd ever have? And how could Don say it so casually, as if it didn't tear him apart, contemplating it.

"If that's all right with you," he said, and she got the impression it wasn't the first time he'd said it.

"Certainly." She flicked a glance at him as he came closer, separated from her now only by the width of the crate. "Do I look like the kind of woman who'd kick out a sick boy? I bet Con's having the time of her life, playing nurse."

Don grinned. "I think she's up there planning about a week's worth of invalid menus, none of which Eric is going to eat gracefully. He's strictly a meat-and-potatoes man."

His smile flickered, then was gone. "As long as the meat is hamburgers and the potatoes are fries."

Tracy managed a weak smile of her own. "I think those are within Con's capabilities."

"Yeah," he said. He leaned back against a workbench, crossed one ankle over the other, folded his arms on his chest, and looked at her. His eyes were hot blue, intense, his mouth a firm line that reminded her of hot kisses, intense passions in the night. And in the morning. Warmth flooded her, licking higher. She swallowed.

"Now," he said softly, uncrossing his legs, "if we are all finished discussing my son and his adventures, dear as the subject is to my heart, will you quit playing with that damned diving suit and come here so I can thank you properly?"

"What—what for?"

He held out a hand to her. "Come here and I'll tell you. Tracy, please. I need to hold you while I . . . do it."

Something in his tone alerted her to his need. She took his hand, let him draw her into his arms, between his legs, let him hold her while she rested against him.

How wonderful it felt to slide her arms around his torso, to hold him, absorb his warmth. She felt a tremor run through him. "You don't have a thing to thank me for," she murmured. "But I need to—"

He cut her off by kissing her hard.

"I have a hell of a lot to thank you for," he said, lifting his head. "But primarily for taking me to Jayne, for getting Eric's picture into that particular newspaper."

His throat worked as he swallowed. His eyes showed his horror of things that might have been. "Eric is convinced the guy wasn't going to bring him here, but was going to take him up to Ketchikan. Once he was back under American jurisdiction, he was going to contact me and say he had my son. He asked a lot of questions about the Meteor Foundation, how much money they might be able to come up with at any given time. Every night, and any time they were in port, he locked Eric up in the compartment he'd stowed away in. Eric overheard him on ship-to-shore talking to somebody in Ketchikan, saying he had a 'valuable cargo' aboard, one that could earn them plenty."

"Don! My God!"

"Yeah," he said. "I told you Eric was too trusting. He must have told the guy every detail of his life, and it was just plain bad luck that he stowed away on the boat of a real old-fashioned opportunist."

"But why did he dump Eric off at Pete's float? And Pete said he did just that. Literally dumped him, shoved him off the boat and left him lying there, threw his bag after him and then was gone so fast, Pete hardly got a good look at the boat."

"Once he read the paper and saw that the police already knew Eric was missing and where he'd been headed, he couldn't take the risk of keeping him aboard." Don shuddered deeply. "I'm just glad he was an opportunist with enough principles to stop short of murder. It would have been easy to dump him overboard a couple of miles from shore."

Tracy held him tightly and they stood in silence for a long time. Finally, she spoke. "Speaking of principles, I want to thank you too." She leaned back against his encircling arms. "You lied for me, Don. I know that can't have been easy. I didn't think you ever lied. I didn't think your moral code permitted it."

"It doesn't, but there comes a time . . ." He shook his head. "You think I'm not aware of the sacrifice you made in inviting all the publicity about Eric?"

"It never occurred to me that there might be publicity when he was found," she said. "And even if it had, I wouldn't have done it differently. It was necessary."

"Not necessary that the poster mention BIO Research," he said.

"Of course it was. This is where you could be reached. This is where we needed to have first word sent."

"Right," he said. "So if you'd tell the truth for me, why wouldn't I lie for you?"

He kissed her until her head swam, then stroked her face with his fingertips. "We have to get back to the house. Con sent me here to find you. I'm supposed to be telling you that she wants you sitting at the table with your fork in your hand before—"

"The gravy boat is filled," Tracy finished with him. "Con's been telling Edie and me that for years. She hates people wandering in late for meals. In a place like this, where things happen and need to be taken care of outside human schedules, she goes crazy. I don't know why she's spent the last twenty years looking after us."

"I do," Don said, brushing another kiss over her mouth. "It's because she loves you. When you love somebody, Tracy, you want to look after them."

She met his gaze and nodded. "That's why I have to protect Dad, even if it means turning down your grant."

Don clenched his teeth and wondered if she was deliberately misunderstanding him, or simply not ready to hear what he wanted to say. He also understood what she was asking so eloquently with those big brown eyes of hers. He had lied for her once. Would he do it again, if only by omission?

"I understand why you need to protect him," he said. "And I won't break your confidence when I report back to the board.

"Now, let's get out of here," he added. "Eric's erroneously convinced that I'm not scared of anything, not even Con. I'd hate to have to burst his bubble."

Tracy thought of the fragile bubble growing inside of her. Don's lying for her had gone a long way toward strengthening it, but it could still be crushed, leaving sharp shards of glass to tear her heart apart. And she still had no idea what his plans were, or how long he meant to stay. Would her love for him have the time it needed to grow strong enough to withstand his absence?

And if it did, did he care enough ever to return to claim it?

With dinner over, Con shoved her chair back. "I'll start changing beds," she said.

"Why?" Tracy looked up from the spear of broccoli lying on her plate in a puddle of congealed cheese sauce.

"Well, I figure sonny boy here's gonna want to be close to his kid, so he better sleep in your room. You can go out to his cottage."

"Thanks, Con," Don said, rising and taking Tracy's plate away from her. "You don't need to change Tracy's sheets on my account."

Tracy stood also, remembering the sheets they'd shared the night before, the scent of them, the scent of Don. She ached, knowing they'd be apart tonight. "Nor his on mine," she said tautly.

Con shrugged. "Fine, then. I'm off home. Sleep well, both of you."

"Fat chance," Don said, turning to look at Tracy from the other side of the room.

"Fat chance," she agreed.

Slowly, carefully, almost soundlessly, he set down the stack of plates he had carried to the sink.

Just as carefully, she set down the items she had picked up from the table.

They met in the middle of the room, clinging together. "I don't suppose you went, uh, shopping today, did you?" he asked.

Tracy shook her head, her face buried against his shoulder. She breathed in the scent of him, felt it go to her head. "I . . . thought about it," she admitted. "I knew you had to stay close to the phone. I had just about convinced myself that I could do it, when Pete got me on the radio."

She lifted her head, laughing softly. "I was intensely relieved that I didn't have to do it. So much for the bold sophistication I thought I'd gained with my years. I was embarrassed merely thinking about going into a small store, in a small community where everyone knows me to make the, uh, purchase.

"And anyway, we couldn't be together tonight, not with Eric sick, needing you close by."

He sighed and kissed her again. "Maybe parenthood isn't everything I've always thought it to be. This has never been a big issue with me before." He squeezed her tightly. "But there'll be other times for us."

Tracy thought it sounded like a question. She hugged him back. "Yes," she said. "Of course there will." But when? And where? As soon as Eric was well, Don had to take him home. And once he was back home, what chance did their relationship have of surviving such a separation?

"I guess," he said, grinning ruefully, "we'd better do the dishes."

There wasn't much of anything else to do, she agreed.

After hanging up the tea towels she'd used, she said, "I'll get a few things from my room, then leave you to it."

Don slid a hand into her hair and kissed her long

and slow. "Yeah. Okay." Then he kissed her short and quick and let her go.

"Do you mind," he asked, following her to her room, lounging in the doorway, "me sleeping in your bed?"

She shook her head, hands locked around her elbows, gaze locked on his. "No." She hated it. She wanted him sleeping in his own bed—with her beside him. Or her sleeping in her own bed—with him *in*side her.

"I wish you could share it with me," he said, looking at it, then back at her.

She didn't move. His hot blue gaze held her pinned. "I know," she whispered.

She watched his throat work as he swallowed. In the silence of the room, she heard him breathing. "Do you . . . do you want that too?" he asked, and the vulnerability, the uncertainty in his expression called out to her.

I've never been so scared in all my life, he'd said the night before. How much courage had it taken for him to admit that depth of insecurity to her? And despite what they'd shared, she could see it still gnawed at him. Was it a result of his ex-wife's infidelity? Did he feel lacking because he hadn't been able to hold her? In essence, he was asking Tracy if he'd "performed" well enough last night for her to want him again.

"Yes," she said, "I want that too." Deep inside, an achy sensation fluttered, then strengthened as she thought of the incredible way he'd performed. She continued to gaze at him. The ache pulsed, spreading heat, threatening the solidity of her knees. Her breathing grew ragged, ineffectual, as she thought about how much she wanted all that he could give her.

He took a step toward her, his face suddenly gaunt and tense. "Are you sure there were only three . . . between us and abstinence?"

She swallowed hard. "Only three. And they're all gone."

"You're not on the pill?" She knew he didn't need an answer to that. He took another step toward her. His fists were clenched at his sides. "Do you suppose you're in a . . . safe part of your cycle?"

She shook her head. "The . . . very worst possible part of it."

He groaned.

She touched the tightly corded tendons of his wrist. "I'm sorry."

He turned his hand and linked their fingers, putting her arm behind her waist and propelling her against him. "Me too," he whispered, and she felt how very sorry he was. It made her even sorrier.

"I guess I better go," she said. She didn't try to move.

"I guess." He didn't release her.

"Just a kiss," he said at length. "Just one kiss won't hurt."

Tracy looked at him. Surely he was right; a goodnight kiss wouldn't hurt.

ELEVEN

"A kiss would be . . . nice," Tracy said.

Don smiled, his lips centimeters from her. "Nice?"

She lowered her lashes, flicked them up again, and moistened her lower lip with the tip of her tongue. He groaned, bending to her, and "nice," she learned, was not the word.

Minutes later she knew how bad a kiss could hurt. One led to another, another, and it escalated from there, from his taking her mouth for just one more, to her somehow ending up on her back on the bed, and him atop her, sucking on her nipples.

Don's heart hammered so hard, he thought it would burst free. He caught Tracy's soft little moans in his mouth, felt her fingertips sink into the muscles of his back. He grasped one of her knees, fitting his hand into the sweet, damp hollow behind it, raising it, making a cradle for himself between her thighs, his hardness against her softness. Their kisses grew wilder, needier, their hands bolder, more desperate in their reaching. Their heartbeats hammered. Their breathing rasped. Their passion escalated.

"Don . . . Don, please!" She moaned, thrashing under him, and he lifted up, stroking his hands over the beautiful flush rising over her breasts and face. She was hot under him, her eyes glazed, her lips parted. She linked her hands behind his head and tried to pull his face down to join her mouth with his. He held off, his arms trembling, praying for strength, but it oozed out of him as she did that thing with the tip of her tongue over her bottom lip again, and slowly opened her lashes, her brown eyes enormous, pleading with him. "Love me," she whispered.

"Oh, God, *baby* . . ." he said raggedly, and lowered himself to her again.

"Dad! Dad! Where are you? Dad, my ears hurt!"

With a curse, Don rolled off Tracy and stood. He looked at her for a moment, at her wanton, trembling limbs, her kiss-swollen mouth, her soft, beseeching eyes, her tousled hair.

Her smile.

"I'll be back," he said, and she nodded.

But when he came back, of course she was gone.

"Eric, I'm sorry, but your mother is right on this one." Tracy heard what had to be the resumption of an argument that had been going on when she'd slipped away to the cabin the previous evening. It seemed Eric was no more reconciled to leaving now than he had been then. He scuffed his feet as he and Don came along the path from the cabin where Don had gone to pack his bag.

She could sympathize. She was no more reconciled to watching Don go now than she had been when he'd announced his decision the night before to leave. But between the Tuesday when he'd arrived, and that Saturday morning, Eric had bounced back to health.

Tracy knew they had to go. She'd known it all along. It just didn't get any easier.

"I'm no more inclined to reward your disobedience than your mother is to let me," Don continued. "Face it, buddy, you screwed up big-time in running away, and there's no way you get to stay. Your ear infection is at a stage now where you're fit to travel."

Eric stomped up onto the porch as Tracy stepped outside. He gave her a look that suggested this was somehow all her fault, and flopped onto a deck chair near where he'd left his green backpack, his long legs thrust out on either side of it. "But I only ever saw one whale, and it was ten miles away!"

"Tough." Don was anything but sympathetic. He left his bag at the bottom of the steps and ascended. "And it was only about a hundred yards off Griffith Point." Eric merely shot him a hate-filled look and turned away to stare out over the water as Don slipped one hand around the back of Tracy's neck.

"Where's Con?" he said softly.

"Con doesn't like saying good-bye."

His fingers moved against her skin. His eyes

searched her face. "Neither do I, Tracy. That's why I'm not going to say it."

She clenched her teeth so her chin wouldn't wobble, firmed her mouth so her lips wouldn't tremble, opened her eyes wide so he wouldn't see the tears she was fighting back.

"Fine," she said. "Then I won't say it either." She'd already said it in her heart, already heard the silvery shattering of blown glass, already felt the bite of its sharp edges. It seemed an added and unnecessary cruelty, having to go through it all again this morning.

It would be easier if the sky had remained gray, if rain had continued to fall as it had over the past two days. If the weather had matched her mood, maybe it wouldn't hurt so bad, watching Don all packed and ready to leave her. The sun shone on his golden hair, burnishing it. It turned his eyes into slices of sky, made his skin look toasty brown, and reminded her of the way it felt.

She didn't want to be reminded.

Why didn't he just go? Why was he putting her through this agony? If she had been able to hide away somewhere and avoid the pain of seeing him leave, she would have. She stepped away from him. He went down the steps, picked up his bag, turned, and looked back at her. "Eric," she said, "your dad's ready to leave."

He cut a sidelong glance at his father. "Yeah, yeah, I see him."

Slowly, so slowly it was almost painful, he got to his feet. Just as slowly, he bent and grabbed at one strap of his pack. He missed and tried again, making a big production out of it, snorting as if the whole thing were someone else's fault, and he merely the innocent bystander who had to pick up the pieces. Heaving the pack over his shoulder, he slouched down the steps to the path.

"You go on down to the boat," Don said. "I'll be with you in a minute."

He bounded back up onto the porch. He was too near. She could feel his heat, his tension, his willing her to look at him. She didn't. She watched Eric stump down the path, each scuffing footstep a reproach aimed at his father. He looked like— She couldn't remember what he reminded her of, but even as she was thinking it, he turned and hollered, "Well, hurry it up! Kiss your girlfriend good-bye and let's go! Mom's waiting, remember? Maybe now you know how *I* feel! She's always calling me home just when I start having fun."

Tracy's throat ached. "You'd better go," she said. "It's not going to be a pleasant trip for you."

He lifted one hand and curled it around her cheek. "Tracy . . . I—" He broke off with a soft curse. "I have to go. I have to take him home. But I'll be back, sweetheart."

She nodded. She didn't believe him. She believed he meant it, but something would intervene, something would prevent his returning. Today would be the last time she'd see him.

"Dammit," he exploded, his hand sliding around

to her nape again. He gripped her tightly. "Tracy, come with me!"

"Come—" She stared at him. "*With you?*" He nodded. Oh, Lord, how she wanted to! Visions swirled though her mind, through her heart, of them together, flying away through the blue sky, headed into a future that until that moment had been something so nebulous, so amorphous, she'd never managed to believe it might be possible. His words gave it form, gave it substance, made it all too real.

A whale broached somewhere, its breath exploding into the air. Tracy backed away from Don. "I . . . can't do that," she whispered. "Don, my father . . . I . . ." She shook her head. "I *can't.*"

He bent and did what his son had suggested, kissed her good-bye, hard and swift and evocative. Then he turned and strode after Eric, who continued on his slow, reluctant way, a kid called home before the fun was over and—

Tracy went rigid as an image flooded her mind. She let out a yell. "Don!" He wheeled back, and she raced down the steps, laughing, crying, shouting.

"I've got it! I've got it! Oh, please, don't go! You have to help me. It's there, somewhere in the tapes we made that day we dove together. It was his mother, calling him home. Remember? We heard it. It has to be on the tapes. If we can find it, amplify it, play it back, *we* can be the ones calling him. We'll call him and he'll come for us, just like he did for her! But I need you here because I promised Edie I'd never dive alone. Don, please, stay, if only for another day!"

"Tracy, calm down. Try to make sense. What are you saying? What are you—"

More slowly, but still tripping over her words in her eagerness, she told him how seeing Eric so reluctant to leave had reminded her of the juvenile whale who'd been the last to leave when they had met the animals underwater. "That was his mother, the distant call we heard just before he left. Don, I'm sure of this! She was calling him back to her. And he went, but he didn't like it. He acted just like Eric. And that call is the one I need. I have to isolate it on the tape, clean it up, amplify it, and play it back."

He gripped her shoulders. His eyes shone. "Holy mackerel," he said slowly. "If we play it back and anyone responds, we'll have identified one specific call as having one specific purpose! You're right! This could be it. We'll need to play the tapes until we find it, then bring it up and—"

He broke off, staring at her in dismay, and Tracy became aware of Eric nearly dancing with excitement, saying, "Can we stay, then, Dad? Can we, huh? Huh?"

"I—no, son, we can't." Don's tone was firm, but his manner as he let his hands fall from Tracy's shoulders held all the reluctance Eric's had only minutes before. "I told your mother that as soon as you were fit to travel, I'd bring you back."

"But she doesn't *know* I'm not dizzy anymore," Eric protested.

"Maybe not," Don said, "but I do."

"But, Dad, you want to stay! You know you do."

Don transferred his gaze from his son to Tracy and

slid his hand under her hair. It was an act of pure possession. "I want it more than anything in the world, but it's not something I can do."

Tracy nodded. She understood.

"If anyone wants my opinion," Con said, startling Tracy, who hadn't known she was there. She turned and saw the old woman standing a few feet away, gazing at the sky, her face blandly innocent. "I figure a kid who's been suffering from dizzy spells should have at least a couple of days—say maybe a weekend—on the water before anyone risks putting him in a car or an airplane to test out his balance. At least aboard a boat, if he needs to puke, he can do it over the side and not mess up nothin'. 'Course, that's just my opinion. Might not be worth a hoot."

Don grabbed her and hugged her, kissed her on the cheek and picked her up, swinging her in a ponderous circle. "Connie, my love, you're a genius, you know that?"

"Put me down, you big, goofy boy!"

Don only laughed and kissed her again.

"Bitchin'," Eric whispered in awe as an orca followed Tracy's kayak into the bay. "Totally bitchin'."

Tracy clambered onto the dock from the frail craft as Don and Eric, in a two-man kayak, swung wide so as not to disturb the animal. Don tore his gaze from Tracy's rapt face and glanced over his shoulder at his son. Eric hadn't stopped filming since the whale first appeared between the two small boats.

"How's she gonna keep it here?" Eric asked, and Don said he didn't suppose she had any intention of keeping it. "Then why'd she bring it home by playing that tape for it?"

"Just, I suppose, to prove to herself that she could." But Tracy, he saw, had something else in mind. Leaving the kayak tied by one end, she gestured to Don to stay where he was. She raced for the house, returned in bare seconds, her flute glinting silver in her hand.

Then, gesturing him in, she murmured, "Pick up the transponder, please. Shut it off." As he paddled close to the end of her kayak and did as she asked, she stood on the edge of the dock, lifted her flute, and played.

The whale rolled to its side, looking at her from one eye, then rolled to the other side and looked at her again. Steadying her mouth, she continued to blow softly across the flute, sending music floating forth, playing anything she could think of, slow music, fast music, hymns, and Christmas carols.

When she swung into "Jingle Bells," the orca fanned its huge tail flukes and rose up out of the water to its full height. Eric let out a yell of delight, then roared with laughter as it fell back down with an exuberant splash.

Before Tracy had finished wiping her face dry, the whale had sounded and was gone. She stood staring out over the water where it had been, wondering if the entire episode had been nothing more than a dream.

Her soaked T-shirt, and Don's hot gaze fixed on it

as he arose from his kayak, told her it had all really happened. He swung her into an embrace, laughing, shouting, congratulating her, dancing her around the dock, and on one of their circuits she saw Eric, still filming madly, focused on her and his father. His grin could have reached around the globe.

"Thank you for staying," she said very early Monday morning. "Thank you for helping me. Thank you for . . ." She glanced at the bedside table, at the foil packages lying empty on the bedside table. "For being so embarrassingly honest when Con asked if there was anything either of us wanted her to pick up in Port McNeill while she was doing her Saturday grocery shopping."

He covered her mouth with his, laughing as he kissed her, still laughing when he lifted his head. "That's something you never have to thank me for, sweetheart. I was rewarded by the look on her face."

Tracy grinned. "That was a moment to remember, wasn't it? But my favorite was when she said, 'Sure, sonny,' then looked at *me* and asked, 'What size?' "

"Yeah, but what about the look on your face when you said to me, 'They come in different sizes?' "

She hid her face against him. "Well, I mean, they stretch, don't they?"

"Good thing too," he murmured. "And you know, there have been other rewards as well for my staying. Several times, if I recall, including this morning."

"And now, since it *is* morning," she said, slipping

away from him and rising from the bed, "I want to get back to my room before your son wakes up."

"Would you mind his knowing?" Don asked. Tracy thought about it while she zipped up her shorts.

She pulled on a sweatshirt. "Yes."

"If we lived together, he'd know. He spends most weekends with me, Tracy."

"We don't live together."

"We could, if you'd come home with me."

She turned to look at him, running her fingers through her hair. "I can't do that. You know I can't. I can't leave my family."

He stood and shoved his legs into his pants, dragging them up over his slim hips. "Then I guess there's nothing more to be said."

Tracy faced him for another minute or two, then said, "No, I guess not."

She slipped out the door. Too upset to go into the house, she entered the bonsai garden. *Live together.* That seemed to be the strongest commitment he was willing to make. *Come home with me*, he said. Only two days ago she had seen those words as giving shape and substance to an indistinct future.

But not now. *Come home with me* and *live with me* were not the same as *marry me.* Okay, it had been only a week. She knew that. But what she didn't know was if that nebulous future would ever mean his saying those words. Never had he used the word *love.* But neither had she. Yet how could she walk away from everything safe, everything secure, from the very certain needs of her father and sister to fulfill whatever needs Don had, when she was still too unclear on what they might actually be.

Ten minutes later Don found her. "Baby, I'm sorry," he said, catching her in his arms and holding her close. "I know I'm not being fair to you, pressuring you this way. Our relationship is too new, yet on some levels I feel as if it's been going on for fifteen years."

He slid his hands into her hair, tilting her face up, his eyes pleading for understanding. "I go wild inside with frustration, thinking of you trapped here, stifled. I worry about you growing rootbound like these stunted little trees of yours. I want to see you grow, expand your horizons, do all the things you've ever dreamed of doing, enjoying all the successes that should be yours."

"I'm sorry too," she said, gripping his wrists. "Sorry that I can't be what you want, can't do what you want. It's what I want too, to be with you, Don, but my family needs me. It's my teaching salary that holds everything together. If I take that away, all of this folds."

"If you accepted the grant money, that wouldn't be an issue."

"I'm not accepting the grant money," she said. "Face it, Don, you can't go back and recommend the award and not tell them about Dad, and I can't let you tell them. Especially not now. You say you want success for me. I've got that. I've succeeded in my greatest aim. I've proved Dad's theory beyond any doubt. I've vindicated him and I'm not going to let anything stand in the way of his getting all the credit."

"All right, I know all that," he said, ramming a hand through his hair as he spun away from her. He thumped his fist atop the mossy wall. "But you could name your own price for that film footage, you know. You could, finally, take your show on the road."

She went to him, slid her arms around him, and pressed her cheek to his back. "That would still mean leaving Dad."

"Is it easier leaving me?"

She wanted to point out that he was the one leaving, but she knew what he meant. "No," she said. "It's no easier. But . . . I can't desert him, or Edie. Don, please give me some time. Let me work things out with them in my own way, in my own time."

"All right," he said, turning and holding her tightly. "But make no mistake, Tracy, we are going to be together. One way or another."

Looking into his eyes, it was almost easy to believe it. But two hours later, watching the wake of his rental boat widen and roll up against the shore, it suddenly became impossible.

TWELVE

The following day, as she was unloading her gear, Tracy looked up in response to the sound of heavy diesel engines to see a forty-foot cruiser rumbling toward the wharf. The boat's name in an elegant scroll across the command bridge—*April Dreaming*—impinged first on her consciousness. She blinked, stared, and blinked again before lifting her gaze to her former brother-in-law's, and beside him, her sister's, laughing face.

"Edie?" she said hollowly, and automatically caught the line cast by Harry, who stood on the bow.

What was Edie doing aboard her ex-husband's father's boat? When she'd spoken to her sister only the day before, there had been no mention of Tom, and no mention either of coming home or bringing Wanda and Harry for a visit. As much as she loved their old friends, Tracy wasn't in the mood to entertain.

As Tom kicked the stern toward the dock, Tracy's

father emerged from the cabin, looking bewildered, followed by Wanda, who grabbed Tracy in a hug as soon as she was aboard.

The professor caught his younger daughter's hand as she descended the ladder to the deck. "Agnes?" he said plaintively. "Who are all these people?"

"Oh, Trace, be happy for me," Edie said later that day. The sisters sat in the bonsai garden, sharing the bench under the tree. "It's been only a few days, and we don't know that it's going to work out for us, but we both want to try. We both want that really badly."

"How did you get together again?"

Edie looked down at her linked fingers. "We . . . just sort of . . . ran into each other and . . . got to talking. It sort of went from there."

"Have you forgiven him?" Tracy asked gently. Infidelity wasn't something she thought she could ever forgive, but . . . If it meant the difference between a life that included Don and one that did not . . . then maybe.

"I believe I can," Edie said. "I'm working on it. We've talked about the period in our lives. A lot. He made a mistake. He knows it and he's sorry. But I made some mistakes too. I neglected him when our marriage was new and vulnerable. Sure, I did it with the best of motives and justified it by saying that Mom and Dad needed me. But what I forgot was that Tom needed me too.

"That's not something I'm going to forget again,"

she said. Then, catching Tracy's hands and squeezing them, she added, "He'd like to spend the rest of the summer here with me if that's okay with you."

"Of course it's okay with me! But you don't need my permission. This is your home too, Edie. And I am glad for you." She hugged her sister. "I hope you and Tom can work it out. I've always liked him, you know, even when I didn't like the things he did, the way he hurt you."

"I know. And I've always loved him, even when I was hurting so bad, the only way I could stay sane was to tell myself I hated him. And he still loves me. He says he never stopped, even when he was . . ." She let it trail off.

Living with Stephanie, Tracy finished silently for her sister. She looked into Edie's eyes and saw there all the hopes and dreams and belief in the future that any woman could ever want.

"I am happy for you," she said, hugging Edie again. "Truly I am. I've worried about you so much these past three years."

"Then you really don't mind? You could use another qualified diver, couldn't you? To say nothing of a carpenter?" Tom was both.

"Of course." She sat back from Edie. "But . . . I—we don't have enough money to put him back on the payroll. I hope he knows that."

Edie shrugged. "He's sold several songs since spring, so things are looking up in that department. If this works out, Tracy, between Tom and me, he's hoping to stay here this winter too, and help me look after

Dad. He's really eager to get at some of the building maintenance that's gotten beyond Con. He can see how badly things have deteriorated in his absence."

"Edie, that would be great, but as I said, we can't put him on the payroll. Would he be willing to stay and not have a real job?" Carpentry had been Tom's original job on Blackfish Island, one he'd done well, but since the divorce and his leaving, none of it had gotten done.

"Uh, Trace," Edie said with a frown, "did Don Jacobs say, um, anything while he was here?"

Tracy looked at her sharply. "About what?"

Edie bit her lip. "Well, about a grant, maybe, from the Meteor Foundation?"

All at once Tracy understood. "You?" she said. "You sent in that grant application in Dad's name?"

Edie jumped up and squealed. "We *got* it? I was scared to tell you after I did it. I didn't want to get your hopes up, but I was so sick of seeing you work your butt off all alone because we had no money to hire a decent staff. Oh, Tracy," she implored, "tell me we got it, or that there's a chance that we will. That's why he came, isn't it, to check us out?"

For the first time in her life, Tracy knew what it meant to see red.

"Yes, we got it," she said between her teeth. Rage made her legs tremble as she stood. "*We* got it. And *I* turned it down!"

"Turned it *down*? Are you crazy?"

"No, dammit, are you?" she shouted. "Edie, don't you know what you did? Don't you know what you risked?" She went on, her voice rising higher and higher, to list all the possibilities she'd so long guarded against, most notably loss of their father's credibility. "I thought you cared about that too! I thought we were working together on protecting Dad! How could you do that to him?"

"To him?" Edie said, her own temper flaring. "Don't you mean to you? It's *your* years of work you're trying to protect, Tracy, not Dad's. Do you think it would hurt him now, anything they might say about him? It wouldn't matter one whit! He doesn't know what anyone says, what anyone thinks, and if he did, he wouldn't care! He never did. It was you, you who were embarrassed by those who scoffed at him, you who felt ashamed when they rejected his theories.

"Well, maybe you think you were trying to protect him from all that, but I was trying to protect you. I love you. You spend so much of your life looking after other people, I figured it was time someone did something for you, but since you don't want it, since you don't appreciate it, since you *turned it down*," she shouted in outrage, "I'll take myself and my father and my husband and get out of your way."

She wheeled and ran out of the garden, into the arms of her ex, who had come to see what all the yelling was about. He gathered her close, shooting a furious glare at Tracy. But before he could lead her away, Edie wrenched herself free and spun to face her sister again.

"Do you know why you want to publish Dad's findings under his name, Tracy? The real reason, not the one you've been telling yourself and everyone else all this time? It's because you're scared stiff that if you try to publish anything under your own name, no one will pay the slightest bit of attention."

Tracy was still there when Edie came creeping back. She sat beside her and put out a tentative hand. Tracy took it, clinging to it as if it were a lifeline.

"I'm sorry," Edie said in a small voice. "Oh, God, Trace, I'm so sorry. Can you forgive me?"

"Sure. But what you said was true."

"No. No, I was just mad, and hurt that you didn't praise me for doing something I thought was pretty clever. And, I guess, in the back of my mind was the idea that if we had enough money, maybe Tom could come back if only to work for us, and then maybe I'd have a chance to get back together with him."

Tracy peered at her in the gathering dusk. "Last December you were thinking about that?"

"I've been thinking about that since the day we split up. Our running into each other was no accident. I . . . engineered it. With Wanda's help. Trace, believe me, I didn't want to hurt you, but I guess I never really understood how strongly you felt about finishing Dad's work. Or even why you felt that way. That's why I said that vicious thing. I know there's a lot more to all you've done than that."

"No, Edie. You said what you did because it's true. We both know it. You saw it sooner than I did, but I'm glad you made me see it too. It's given me a lot to think about."

After her sister left her there again, Tracy continued to sit. Don had said he feared seeing her grow stunted, rootbound like one of the bonsai shrubs.

That was what she was in danger of doing. He was right. With the grant money, she could get away. And Edie was right, it wouldn't matter one iota to her father what anyone said. And he did not need Tracy at all. If she left, he wouldn't miss her, wouldn't notice she was gone. She was away all winter at the university anyway, and it never put so much as a ripple in his life.

Neither did Edie need her.

The fact was, she needed them. She had felt safest in her own little sphere where she could feel important. She was afraid of change. Afraid of taking chances. She wasn't the brave big sister, the take-charge one who held the family together. She was a coward who held her loved ones around her like a shield against a world that might reject her.

She went inside and looked in on her father. He lay on his side, his face relaxed in sleep, one hand curled under his cheek like a child. She bent and kissed him. "Good-bye, Daddy. I should have said it a long time ago, shouldn't I, when you said it to me by forgetting who I am."

She knocked on her sister's door gently, so as not to disturb them if they slept. Edie came to the door, opening it wide. She'd been lying in bed alone. "Come on in," she said, then answered the question Tracy hadn't asked. "Tom's sleeping aboard the boat. We haven't progressed that far yet. I told you, we're taking it slow."

Tracy nodded, then gestured toward the dresser. "While I'm away, you might find you need some . . . certain supplies that you kept under your panties. I saw them when I was helping you pack, and I swiped 'em one night when Don was here."

Edie's eyes widened, china blue and enormous. "Well!" she said. "Well, well, w— Away? Where are you going?"

"San Diego," she said. "First thing in the morning."

"And what are you going to do there?"

Tracy shrugged. "I don't know. I guess maybe I'm taking my show on the road."

It was a long road—three weeks long—and the longest segment by far was the walk across Don's office, with the warm California sun pouring through the slats of the blinds, making stripes of molten gold across his hair, leaving the rest burnished bronze.

"Have a ch—" he said, looking up. His face paled visibly. "Tracy!" He was on his feet, around the desk, reaching for her when she stepped back and put his visitor's chair between them.

"No," she said. "That's not why I'm here. I believe your secretary announced Miss Anderson."

"Excuse me," he said, hurt showing in his eyes. His voice went frigid. "You aren't Tracy. Of course I see that now. Miss Anderson, is it? I assume you must be she?"

Tracy swallowed. This had been a stupid idea, one conceived in desperation. "Don, I'm sorry. I had to do it this way. I had to see you, but it had to be . . . an official visit."

He said nothing, and she finally asked, "May I proceed?"

He nodded. She reached into her capacious shoulder bag and withdrew a large brown envelope. "I brought this for you to read. I hope you'll accord me the same time you'd give my fictitious Miss Anderson if she really were here, and treat what you read with the same degree of consideration. Would you prefer me to wait outside?"

He took the envelope and went behind his desk. "Sit down." He flicked a glance over her. "Miss Anderson."

Tracy watched Don as he stood for another moment or two before resuming his seat. He wore a lightweight gray suit with a pale green shirt, a navy tie with a fine burgundy stripe. It was, she realized with a start as he sat down, the first time she had seen him in anything but the most casual of clothes.

She took a seat in his visitor's chair, and he glanced up from his perusal of the portfolio. His gaze swept over her pale yellow dress, then clung for a moment to her knees, her lower legs, her feet in cream-colored pumps. It was the first time he had seen her in a dress, she supposed.

He looked back down.

Tracy waited.

Traffic rumbled on the street below. Somewhere, a siren screamed. Something hummed quietly in the background. One side of the computer screen on Don's desk was visible to Tracy. It glowed blue. Small silver dots spun across it. She watched them until she was dizzy. A fly buzzed against the window and finally escaped between two slats of the blind. It landed on the back of a green sofa on the other side of the room.

Tracy let her gaze rest on Don's bent head, fascinated by the way two tufts of hair at his crown stuck straight up and fluttered in the faint breeze from the air-conditioning vent over his desk. She looked at his hands, one lying on his blotter, the other holding the edge of a page. He turned it over onto the stack he'd already read. She looked away for five or six minutes, and when she glanced back, he was turning the last page over. He picked up the stack, bounced its ends on the desk to square it, and slipped the pages back inside the envelope. Then he looked at her.

His eyes told her nothing. "I'll see that this is brought to the attention of the other members of the board, Miss Anderson. You have videotapes too, I believe?"

She pulled two out of her bag and set them on the corner of her desk. She rose. "Thank you, Mr. Jacobs."

She thought she saw a smile lurking at the corners of his mouth, but with a stripe of bright light casting an angle across his face, she couldn't be sure. It might have been a grimace of pain.

"Where will you be staying?"

She named the hotel.

"Someone will be in touch with you," he said, and Tracy nodded, closed her bag, and left.

She went back to her hotel, stood looking out the window at a roof garden below, at an elegant, multi-storied shopping arcade half a block away, at the traffic streaming around the corner and out of sight.

She had been there a full three hours when he came.

She knew it was him. There was no doubt in her mind, and she flung open the door to let him in.

He caught her in his arms as he kicked it shut, and then just stood, holding her, one arm around her back, his other hand under her braid, possessing her. His heart hammered so hard, she could feel it through his ribs. A long time later he tilted her face up and looked at her.

"I missed you," he said. "I phoned you . . . so many times I lost count. And your sister would say only that you were away. She wouldn't tell me where. She wouldn't tell me when you'd be back. She wouldn't tell me a damned thing and Con—I thought Con was my friend, but she wouldn't even talk to me! I've been crazy, worrying about you. Oh, baby, you'll never know how much I missed you."

"Yes, I will," she said, sliding her fingers through his hair. "I do. It's the same way I missed you."

"I want to kiss you, Trace." He continued to gaze at her.

She lowered her lashes, parted her lips, and waited.

A second later she let her lashes flutter up again. "So . . . why aren't you doing it?" she asked.

He laughed. "Because if I do, we won't get any talking done. And we do have to talk."

"I know," she said, fluttering her lashes outrageously. "Later . . ."

"I'm so very, very proud of you," he said later—a lot later. "Your films have a wonderfully professional look about them."

"They should," she told him. "They were put together by one of the top film editing companies in Los Angeles. I've spent the last three weeks working with them. I'd have liked to have hired a professional narrator, but the editing job took us right down to the bottom of not only our family barrel, but Harry and Wanda's too. They have faith in me. They look upon it as an investment."

"I don't think their faith is misplaced." He ran a fingertip down her nose and across her mouth, tapping her chin. "And your narration is wonderful. The other members who've read the grant your sister wrote on your behalf, and who've seen the tapes, were impressed, Tracy. That doesn't mean you're in, but under the circumstances, BIO Research having turned down the other one, there is funding left unallocated."

"It doesn't matter, Don. It'd be nice to have it. It would . . . smooth things for us, and that's why I let Edie apply. But I've hired an agent and she's negotiating with a production company that makes and sells documentaries. They're interested in a lot of the other footage I've gathered over the years. The revenue from that, and from the lecture fees I hope to receive, will support BIO Research quite well. And there are other funding bodies."

He rolled apart from her. "What you're saying is that you don't need me."

She sat up, swung her legs over the edge of the mattress, and reached for something to put on. His shirt came to hand. She slipped into it.

"That's right," she said. "I don't need you as a means to gaining funding for BIO Research. But I do need you in so many other capacities, I can't begin to count them. I love you, Don. I want to be with you. Live with you, if that's what you still want."

He stood and dragged on his briefs. Facing her from the other side of the bed, he said very softly, "What did you say?"

She didn't bother playing the game of repeating everything, but gave him the one thing she knew he wanted to hear. "I love you."

She held up a hand as he came around the end of the bed. "It's all right. You don't have to say it back. It's enough for now that you want me." She smiled. "I like having you want me. It's something, you'll remember, that I've worked at since a long time ago. Maybe someday you'll be able to say you love me too, but not until you're ready."

"Not until I'm—what gives you the idea I'm not ready?"

"Because it's so soon, Don, too soon for you to

make that kind of commitment. I know it and accept it. Even when you were trying to convince me to come here and live with you, you didn't claim to love me, and I'm glad of that. If you had, it might not have been possible for me to refuse. And it would have been wrong of me—wrong for me—to go with you then. First I had to figure myself out, discover what it was holding me back from taking what I wanted from life."

Don's shoulders ached from tension as he listened to her explain the things she'd come to understand about herself, with her sister's help. He wanted to tell her that Edie had been wrong, but how could he, when he, too, knew she was right. But how it must have hurt Tracy to hear it. He should have been there for her, to help her over those emotional hurdles. He should have been, and he had not.

He turned away from her and stood in the tall, narrow window looking down at the roof garden. He struggled for words, knew that whatever he said would be inadequate to express everything he felt, but knew that he had to try. He owed her that.

"I wanted to say it," he said. "I wanted to, and yet, I didn't want to."

He turned, letting the sheer curtains fall into place behind him. "Once," he said, "I told a woman I loved her when I did not. I lived with that lie long enough that I began to believe it was the truth, the same way I believed the lie she told when she said she loved me. This time, I needed to be sure. Of myself, yes, but of you too.

"It became more important to me that *you* showed me you were willing to make a commitment—to me, to our relationship—before I showed you how . . . vulnerable I felt.

"I said I wanted to be there for you, but when it came right down to the crunch, I wasn't, was I? You were just as scared, just as vulnerable, and I left you not knowing how I feel about you."

He searched her face, hoping to see some sign that she was with him, that she understood, but all he saw was that calm intelligence he had come to expect from her, the quiet expectance that seemed, oddly, to have no expectations.

"I do love you, Tracy," he said hoarsely, taking a step toward her. "I think I fell in love with you six years ago, but I didn't recognize it then. I was intrigued by your new maturity, fascinated by your fire, your enthusiasm, your passion for what you believed in.

"But it wasn't until I went to Blackfish Island last month that I knew for sure I wanted all of that passion of yours directed at me on a very intense and personal level. When I felt it, when I held you in my arms and felt you respond to my kiss that first day, and later when I made love with you, I knew I loved you as I never hoped to love any woman. Yet I didn't feel safe with it, so I used your desire to look after your family as an excuse to leave without telling you how I felt, for fear you'd reject what I offered, just the way I rejected you once."

She glided across the room until their bodies

nearly touched. "You said I never had to worry about that again from you. You don't ever have to worry about it from me. I want you. I won't want any other man. I won't have any other man. If it's not you, it's no one."

He slipped his fingertips inside the front of her shirt and parted the garment, watching a faint anticipatory pucker of her nipples. It dried his mouth and slicked his hands. "Live with me," he said, capturing her gaze with his. "Marry me."

She stared at him; he watched her mouth part on a soundless word. Her lashes dropped to hide her suddenly glowing eyes, then lifted again, revealing concerns, doubts, he didn't want her to have. "Don't you think it's too soon for either of us to make that kind of commitment?" she asked.

He thought for a moment. "Yes," he said honestly. "Do you?"

She nodded, and he saw that glow resume in her eyes, saw the smile curving her plump red, kissable lips. "Much too soon," she said, and swayed against him.

He caught her, lifted her up until her legs wrapped around his waist. "But are we going to let that stop us?" he said, walking to the side of the bed and sitting with her astride his lap.

"Never!" she said, and flung herself back against the restraining band of his arms, her hair flying out behind her. She laughed joyously, full of certainty and power and enthusiasm. "We're not going to let anything stop us!"

Then, swinging upright, she pressed on his shoulders, her motion carrying them both backward onto the mattress. Lying on him, her hair draped around her face and his, she whispered, "Is this where I get that full body massage?"

It was.

THE EDITOR'S CORNER

Spring is on its way, and with it come four wonderful new LOVESWEPTs. You'll want to lose yourself in these terrific stories with funny, interesting and sexy characters written by some of the most talented authors writing women's fiction today.

Starting things off is the ever-popular Charlotte Hughes with **HUSBAND WANTED,** LOVESWEPT #734. Fannie Brisbane knows it is an impossible scheme, but unless she agrees to it, the daughter she gave up for adoption years ago will know the truth, that she's not rich and married! Her Griddle and Grill customers all pitch in, offering clothes, even a mansion—but when Clay Bodine offers to play her husband, Fannie doesn't know if she should dare say yes to a charade with the man who's always owned her heart. With her trademark humor and unforgettable characters, Charlotte delivers another sweetly sizzling romance that resonates with tenderness and sparkles with fun.

Linda Cajio's heroine has found **THE PERFECT CATCH,** LOVESWEPT #735. Elaine Sampson cheers joyfully, waving her arms as the player rounds the bases—and drenches the gorgeous guy in front of her with ice and cola! Graham Reed accepts her apology, but when the pretty teacher follows him to the men's room to help clean his suit, he laughs . . . and wonders if he is falling in love. He makes her reckless, kisses her senseless, but this handsome hunk might be a little out of her league. Linda's delightful love story hits an out-of-the-park home run!

Welcome Faye Hughes, a wonderfully talented new writer debuting at Loveswept with **CAN'T FIGHT THE FEELING,** LOVESWEPT #736. It took Justin Stone five minutes to fall in love with Morgan Tremayne—and nearly six years to recover from their quickie divorce ten months later! Now Morgan is back—flirting, teasing, igniting desires that have never really died—and determined to show her beloved pirate that she is his destiny. Once he wooed her with poetry and kisses that melted her clothes off, but now he wants to claim his fallen angel at last. Wildly sexy and delightfully outrageous, this sensational novel by Faye will enchant readers with a story that's as playful as it is seductive.

Last but not least is the fabulous Linda Warren with **AFTER MIDNIGHT,** LOVESWEPT #737. Cord Prescott never asks if Arianna Rossini is guilty when he comes to bail her out of jail, but something unspoken passes between them and tells him she didn't embezzle the missing money. But when she asks for a deal instead of a trial, he aches to learn her secrets, to persuade her to surrender the truth. Consumed by desire, haunted by guilt, Ari must help Cord make peace with his own demons. In a novel that's all at once provocative, passionate, and poignant, Linda explores a forbidden love between a rebel attorney who's won everything but a woman's heart and a lady whose mystery may be innocence or deceit.

Happy reading!

With warmest wishes,

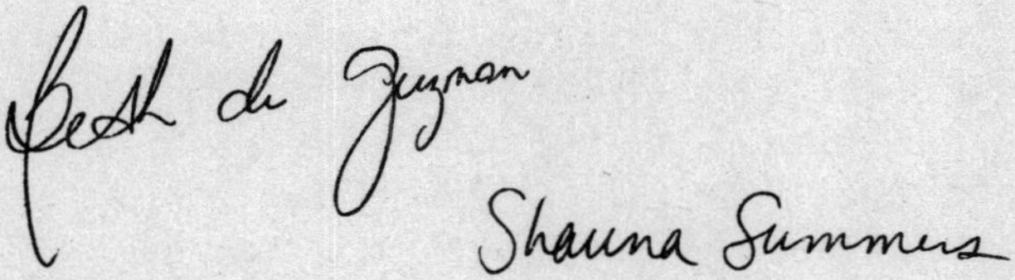

Beth de Guzman | Shauna Summers
Senior Editor | Assistant Editor

P.S. Don't miss the women's novels coming your way in April: **MISTRESS,** by Amanda Quick, is the terrific *New York Times* bestseller, in paperback for the first time; **DANGEROUS TO KISS,** by the award-winning Elizabeth Thornton, is an unforgettable historical romance in the tradition of Amanda Quick and Jane Feather, set in Regency England; **LONG NIGHT MOON,** by highly acclaimed author

Theresa Weir, is a gripping and emotional romance in which a brash reporter helps an ethereal beauty escape a harrowing life. And immediately following this page, look for a preview of the exciting romances from Bantam that are *available now!*

"A master of the genre."
—*Publishers Weekly*

NIGHT SINS

by

TAMI HOAG

Available in Hardcover

Every once in a while a thriller comes along that stretches the limits of the genre and takes readers places they have never been before. Night Sins *is such a novel. . . .*

Deer Lake is a small Minnesota town where people know their neighbors and crime is something that happens on the evening news. But the illusion of safety is shattered when eight-year-old Josh Kirkwood disappears from a hockey rink as he waits for his mother to pick him up after practice. The only thing the police find is his duffel bag with a note stuffed inside: ignorance is not innocence but SIN.

The following is a chilling preview of what transpires the night Hannah realizes her son is missing.

"I forgot. I forgot he was waiting."

A fresh wave of tears washed down Hannah's

cheeks and fell like raindrops onto the lap of her long wool skirt. She doubled over, wanting to curl into a ball while the emotions tore at her. Mitch leaned closer and stroked her hair, trying to offer some comfort. The cop in him remained calm, waiting for facts, reciting the likely explanations. Deeper inside, the parent in him experienced a sharp stab of instinctive fear.

"When I g-got to the rink he w-was g-gone."

"Well, honey, Paul probably picked him up—"

"No. Wednesday is *my* night."

"Did you call Paul to check?"

"I tried, but he wasn't in the office."

"Then Josh probably got a ride with one of the other kids. He's probably at some buddy's house—"

"No. I called everyone I could think of. I checked at the sitter's—Sue Bartz. I thought maybe he would be there waiting for me to come pick up Lily, but Sue hadn't seen him." And Lily was still there waiting for her mother, probably wondering why mama had come and gone without her. "I checked at home, just in case he decided to walk. I called the other hockey moms. I drove back to the rink. I drove back to the hospital. *I can't find him.*"

"Do you have a picture of your son?" Megan asked as she came around the desk.

"His school picture. It's not the best—he needed a haircut, but there wasn't time." Hannah pulled her purse up onto her lap. Her hands shook as she dug through the leather bag for her wallet. "He brought the slip home from school and I made a note, but then time just got away from me and I— forgot."

She whispered the last word as she opened to the

photograph of Josh. *I forgot.* Such a simple, harmless excuse. Forgot about his picture. Forgot about his haircut. Forgot him. Her hand trembled so badly she could barely manage to slip the photograph from the plastic window. She offered it to the dark-haired woman, realizing belatedly that she had no idea who the woman was.

"I'm sorry," she murmured, dredging up the ingrained manners and a fragile smile. "Have we met?"

Mitch sat back against the edge of the desk again. "I'm sorry, Hannah. This is Agent O'Malley with the Bureau of Criminal Apprehension. Megan, this is Dr. Hannah Garrison, head of the emergency room in our community hospital. One of the best doctors ever to wield a stethoscope," he added with a ghost of a grin. "We're very lucky to have her."

Megan studied the photograph, her mind on business, not social niceties. A boy of eight or nine wearing a Cub Scout uniform stared out at her. He had a big gap-toothed grin and a smattering of freckles across his nose and cheeks. His hair was an unruly mop of sandy brown curls. His blue eyes were brimming with life and mischief.

"Is he normally a pretty responsible boy?" Megan asked. "Does he know to call you if he's going to be late or to get permission to go to a friend's house?"

Hannah nodded. "Josh is very levelheaded."

"What did he wear to school today?"

Hannah rubbed a hand across her forehead, trying to think back to morning. It seemed as much a dream as any of this, long ago and foggy. Lily crying at the indignity of being confined to her high chair. Josh skating around the kitchen floor in his stocking feet. Permission slip needed signing for a field trip to the Science Museum. Homework done? Spelling words memorized? A call from the hospital. French toast burning on the stove. Paul storming around the kitchen, snapping at Josh, complaining about the shirts that needed ironing.

"Um—jeans. A blue sweater. Snow boots. A ski jacket—bright blue with bright yellow and bright green trim. Um . . . his Viking stocking cap—it's yellow with a patch sewn on. Paul wouldn't let him wear a purple one with that wild coat. He said it would look like Josh was dressed by color-blind gypsies. I couldn't see the harm; he's only eight years old . . ."

Megan handed the photograph back and looked up at Mitch. "I'll call it in right away." Her mind was already on the possibilities and the steps they should take in accordance with those possibilities. "Get the bulletin to your people, the sheriff's department, the highway patrol—"

Hannah looked stricken. "You don't think—"

"No," Mitch interceded smoothly. "No, honey, of course not. It's just standard procedure. We'll put out a bulletin to all the guys on patrol so if they see Josh they'll know to pick him up and bring him home.

"Excuse us for just a minute," he said, holding up a finger. He turned his back to Hannah and a furious look to Megan. "I need to give Agent O'Malley a few instructions."

He clamped a hand on Megan's shoulder and herded her unceremoniously out the door and into the narrow, dimly-lit hall. A round-headed man in a tweed blazer and chinos gave them a dirty look and stuck a finger in his free ear as he tried to have a conversation on a pay phone outside the men's room door. Mitch hit the phone's plunger with two fingers, cutting off the conversation and drawing an indignant "Hey!" from the caller.

"Excuse us," Mitch growled, flashing his badge. "Police business."

He shouldered the man away from the phone and sent him hustling down the hall with a scowl that had scattered petty drug pushers and hookers from the meanest streets in Miami. He turned the same scowl on Megan. He towered over her and had to outweigh her by a good eighty pounds. He had physically intimidated men who were twice her size and mean as alligators. Yet she glared right back at him.

"What the hell is wrong with you?" she snapped, jumping on the offensive, knowing it was her best defense. She could feel his temper, a physical heat that seared her skin.

"What the hell is wrong with me?" Mitch barked, keeping his voice low. "What the hell is wrong with you—scaring the poor woman—"

"She has reason to be scared, Chief. Her son is missing."

"That has yet to be established. He's probably playing at a friend's house."

"She says she checked with his friends."

"Yes, but she's panicked. She's probably forgotten to look in an obvious place."

"Or somebody grabbed the kid."

Mitch scowled harder because it took an effort to

dismiss her suggestion outright. "This is Deer Lake, O'Malley, not New York."

Megan arched a brow. "You don't have crime in Deer Lake? You have a police force. You have a jail. Or is that all just window dressing?"

"Of course we have crime," he snarled. "We have college students who shoplift and cheese factory workers who get drunk on Saturday night and try to beat each other up in the American Legion parking lot. We don't have child abductions, for Christ's sake."

"Yeah, well, welcome to the nineties, Chief," she said sarcastically. "It can happen anywhere."

"Power, passion, tragedy, and triumph are Rosanne Bittner's hallmarks. Again and again, she brings readers to tears."
—*Romantic Times*

THE FOREVER TREE

by

Rosanne Bittner

Against the glorious, golden land of California, award-winning Rosanne Bittner creates another sweeping saga of passion, tragedy, and adventure . . . as a Spanish beauty and a rugged New Englander struggle against all odds to carve out an empire—and to forge a magnificent love.

Here is a look at this powerful novel.

Señorita Lopez, what are you doing here alone?"

"I often come here," Santana answered. "*Mi padre* lets me go riding alone, as long as it is only to this place that he knows I love." She looked up at the lone pine tree. "I hope that you would never cut this tree, or those around it that protect and shelter it. I feel sorry for it. It seems so alone here, so I come to keep it company. I call it my forever tree."

"The forever tree. Why is that?"

She shrugged. "When I think about how old the California pines become, and how young this one still is, I know it will be here for a very long time, long after I die, even though I am only sixteen." Will saw a shadow of sadness cross her face. "So many things in life change as we grow older, but a tree is forever, a sign that some things never have to change."

He frowned, touched by the way she described the tree as something with a heart and soul. That was how he felt about trees himself, that they were a form of living poetry, something strong yet warm, something that gave so many things to man—shade, homes, paper, the warmth of a wood fire . . . "I'm glad to know you love trees as much as I do," he answered. He was sure he was not supposed to be alone with her this way, but he didn't care. She wore no veil, no special jewelry. Like the day she had come to his room, she was simply dressed. She needed nothing to add to her beauty.

"I love trees very much, *señor*, and the birds, the animals . . ."

Will smiled. "I wish you would just call me Will."

Santana felt a flush coming to her cheeks. "It is best that I do not," she said, smiling shyly. "Well, perhaps whenever I see you alone this way."

Will wondered if that meant she wanted to meet alone with him more often. That did not seem wise, but then, she was too young to be wise, and he was too enamored with her when she was near like this to care about doing the wise thing himself. "Good," he answered. "I have enjoyed getting to know you and your family, Santana. May I call you Santana?"

"*Si*, when we are alone."

Will looked her over, thinking how lovely her naked body must be under her dark riding habit. "I doubt that will happen very often."

She shrugged. "I suppose not. You will be very busy soon with building your mill, and I will be busy with my schooling, and with preparing myself for marriage."

He caught the bitterness in her words. "Surely you don't really want to marry Hugo Bolivar."

She turned away. "That is a forbidden subject."

Will sighed. "All right then, what *can* we talk about?" A little voice warned him that he should get on his horse and ride hell-bent out of there. A stronger force, though, made him stay. For more than two weeks now he had argued with himself that he should keep out of this woman's business, but every time he saw her at meals, listened to her talk, realized what a lovely and innocent woman-child she was, he felt anger and frustration at the thought of her becoming Hugo's wife.

Their eyes met. "*Gracias*," she said. "You are a very nice man, Will Lassater. I like talking with you. You make it easy. I can never find anything to talk about with Hugo. He only likes to talk about himself and his riches." She looked away, realizing she had said something she had not meant to say. "I suppose I will get used to him. Once he is my husband, we will have many things to talk about, and there will be children to share."

A pain stabbed through Will's gut at the thought

of Bolivar bedding Santana. He had no doubt the man would be rough and demanding. "You don't really want to marry that man and have children by him, do you?"

Santana rose, walking a few feet away. "I told you I cannot talk about that. I should not have even mentioned him."

"Nobody knows we're talking about it. Something tells me you *need* to talk about it, Santana. Probably nobody else you know understands how much you detest marrying Hugo. They all think you should be honored and privileged to marry such a man. But you don't want to, do you?"

MY GUARDIAN ANGEL

Five bewitching tales of romance from

Sandra Chastain Kay Hooper
Susan Krinard Karyn Monk
Elizabeth Thornton

ALMOST AN ANGEL by Kay Hooper
A handsome British agent won't rest until he finds the beautiful stranger who miraculously rescued him—then vanished as quickly as she appeared.

GUARDIAN OF THE HEART by Sandra Chastain
A brave young widow is left alone to fend for herself on the banks of the Rio Grande, until the ghost of her husband brings her a second chance at love.

ANGEL ON MY SHOULDER by Susan Krinard
A lovely actress torn from her lover's arms finds that her beloved pet, a wily parrot, houses a spirit determined to see that the two meet again.

SAVING CELESTE by Karyn Monk
A Bostonian with a tragic past prevents a despairing young woman from throwing herself off a bridge, and discovers that she holds the key to his happiness.

THE TROUBLE WITH ANGELS
by Elizabeth Thornton
The rakish young footman from Dangerous to Love *makes a reappearance, this time dancing attendance on a spoiled beauty bent on landing a titled husband. It's all Flynn can do to keep his charge's reputation intact—and his hands to himself.*

"Fresh, exciting . . . wonderfully sensual . . . sure to be noticed in the romance genre."
—Amanda Quick

PAGAN BRIDE

by

Tamara Leigh

Bound by the chains of slavery in an exotic land, Lucien de Gautier had only one chance of escape. In exchange for his freedom, he pledged to smuggle a virtuous young woman out of a harem and onto a ship bound for England. But Lucien couldn't know that the real danger would lie not in the long voyage ahead, but in his dazzling charge: a ravishing innocent whose flame-red hair and emerald eyes would unleash his most potent desires. . . .

The music grew louder, its vigorous beat coursing through every vein in every limb that moved to it. Tightly, it wound itself around the slender woman who swayed at the center of the large room. It pulled her head back and closed her eyes against the light. It drew her arms up from her sides and spread them wide to embrace the sensual rhythm she had given herself over to. It shook her shoulders, rotated and jerked her hips, and caused her fingers to snap.

The female dancers who had been hired to entertain the women of Abd al-Jabbar's harem drifted away, going to stand along the walls and watch this strange one who had joined in the dance.

She was different from the other women, her hair a flame amid the ashes. Skin that should have been pale was tanned and faintly touched with freckles. Though fine-boned and slim, her body curved where it ought to, her breasts full and firm. And those pale green eyes—they were full of daring and laughter when she turned them upon her captive audience.

All watched as the tempo quickened and the solitary dancer swept across the floor, sparkling laughter spilling from her throat as the music pulled her deeper into its spell.

Unmindful of the pins holding her veil in place, the young woman snatched the translucent material from her waist-length hair and drew it taut between her hands. Then, raising her arms above her head, she pivoted on the balls of her bare feet. Faster and faster she turned, until she whirled in the wake of the diaphanous material clothing her limbs.

More laughter parted her lips, followed by a shriek of delight as the music reached its zenith. She was lost in it—completely given over to its control.

"Alessandra!" A reproving voice split the air.

The music fell away, and a din of women's voices rose to take its place.

Wrenched from the trancelike state she had slipped into, Alessandra staggered around to face her mother's displeasure. However, the room continued to revolve as if she were still dancing.

She sank to her knees and sat back on her heels, the dizziness making it impossible for her to focus on the woman who stood at the far end of the room.

Standing betwen Sabine and Khalid, Lucien knew he was in trouble. He had known the moment Sabine had called out to the wild dancer, naming her the one. Inwardly, he groaned and cursed his man's flesh. One look at the young woman as she whirled across the floor was all it had taken to decide him. Thinking her a dancer—though with her mother's hair falling down her back, he should have known otherwise—he had determined to have her as soon as possible. Then the accursed woman at his side had shattered the possibility. Or had she?

OFFICIAL RULES **NO PURCHASE NECESSARY**

To enter the sweepstakes outlined below, you must respond by the date specified and follow all entry instructions published elsewhere in this offer.

DREAM COME TRUE SWEEPSTAKES

Sweepstakes begins 9/1/94, ends 1/15/96. To qualify for the Early Bird Prize, entry must be received by the date specified elsewhere in this offer. Winners will be selected in random drawings on 2/29/96 by an independent judging organization whose decisions are final. Early Bird winner will be selected in a separate drawing from among all qualifying entries.

Odds of winning determined by total number of entries received. Distribution not to exceed 300 million.

Estimated maximum retail value of prizes: Grand (1) $25,000 (cash alternative $20,000); First (1) $2,000; Second (1) $750; Third (50) $75; Fourth (1,000) $50; Early Bird (1) $5,000. Total prize value: $86,500.

Automobile and travel trailer must be picked up at a local dealer; all other merchandise prizes will be shipped to winners. Awarding of any prize to a minor will require written permission of parent/guardian. If a trip prize is won by a minor, s/he must be accompanied by parent/legal guardian. Trip prizes subject to availability and must be completed within 12 months of date awarded. Blackout dates may apply. Early Bird trip is on a space available basis and does not include port charges, gratuities, optional shore excursions and onboard personal purchases. Prizes are not transferable or redeemable for cash except as specified. No substitution for prizes except as necessary due to unavailability. Travel trailer and/or automobile license and registration fees are winners' responsibility as are any other incidental expenses not specified herein.

Early Bird Prize may not be offered in some presentations of this sweepstakes. Grand through third prize winners will have the option of selecting any prize offered at level won. All prizes will be awarded. Drawing will be held at 204 Center Square Road, Bridgeport, NJ 08014. Winners need not be present. For winners list (available in June, 1996), send a self-addressed, stamped envelope by 1/15/96 to: Dream Come True Winners, P.O. Box 572, Gibbstown, NJ 08027.

THE FOLLOWING APPLIES TO THE SWEEPSTAKES ABOVE:

No purchase necessary. No photocopied or mechanically reproduced entries will be accepted. Not responsible for lost, late, misdirected, damaged, incomplete, illegible, or postage-die mail. Entries become the property of sponsors and will not be returned.

Winner(s) will be notified by mail. Winner(s) may be required to sign and return an affidavit of eligibility/release within 14 days of date on notification or an alternate may be selected. Except where prohibited by law, entry constitutes permission to use of winners' names, hometowns, and likenesses for publicity without additional compensation. Void where prohibited or restricted. All federal, state, provincial, and local laws and regulations apply.

All prize values are in U.S. currency. Presentation of prizes may vary; values at a given prize level will be approximately the same. All taxes are winners' responsibility.

Canadian residents, in order to win, must first correctly answer a time-limited skill testing question administered by mail. Any litigation regarding the conduct and awarding of a prize in this publicity contest by a resident of the province of Quebec may be submitted to the Regie des loteries et courses du Quebec.

Sweepstakes is open to legal residents of the U.S., Canada, and Europe (in those areas where made available) who have received this offer.

Sweepstakes in sponsored by Ventura Associates, 1211 Avenue of the Americas, New York, NY 10036 and presented by independent businesses. Employees of these, their advertising agencies and promotional companies involved in this promotion, and their immediate families, agents, successors, and assignees shall be ineligible to participate in the promotion and shall not be eligible for any prizes covered herein. SWP 3/95